A FRENCH DECEPTION THRILLER

A Forgery in Toulouse

BOOK FOUR IN A SERIES

JANICE NAGOURNEY

CASTLE BRIDGE MEDIA
DENVER, COLORADO, USA

CASTLE BRIDGE MEDIA
Denver, Colorado

Cover photo by H Cluzeaud/Wikimedia Commons.
This photo has been modified.

This book is a work of fiction. Names, characters, business, events, and incidents are the products of the authors' imaginations. Any resemblance to actual persons, living or dead or actual events is purely coincidental.

ISBN: 979-8-9940410-0-0

To Tom

Per Tolosa totjorn mai

For Toulouse always more

FRENCH DECEPTION:
A FORGERY IN TOULOUSE

PROLOGUE

January 2011

IT WASN'T THE FIRST TIME he'd been hustled away like this, but it ought to be the last. So reflected the passenger as the car he was seated in—a gray Citröen that had seen better days—pulled onto the highway.

Old age had weakened his legs and lungs, but his mind remained intact. Today, as they often did, visions of the boys passed through his mind. At the same time, the memories of other trips to safety were vivid, as though they'd taken place only yesterday.

As for the boy—of course, he was no longer a boy—he'd recognized him even before he'd opened his mouth to speak. Those eyes—empty of emotion, daring you to guess what he was thinking. How had he found him? And why was he coming around complaining at this late date? Now that he thought about it, he remembered the boy's mother, thanking him for taking such good care of her son. As he had, in his own way. She'd even defended him when some of the other parents complained, but he'd been sent to another diocese anyway. Not that that mattered; he'd continued to satisfy his needs in one school after another until he was eventually transferred back to *Saint-Bernard* where there were no longer any boys.

The driver headed west toward Clermont-Ferrand, and a few kilometers out, the traffic ground to a halt as roadworks siphoned the vehicles into a single lane. Despite the slow crawl, three cars had managed to create a major collision—the sort of feat that some people spent long years training for until they could pull it off. With the engine idling, the air in the car grew stuffy; JP lowered his window to let in an icy blast, tinged with the smell of the highway. The shapeless black form seated in the rear coughed, then snapped at the driver, 'Close the window, I'm freezing to death back here."

If only. "Of course, Father, we just needed to get a bit of fresh air."

They inched past the accident, the roadworks ended, and they drove west, then headed south after passing by Clermont-Ferrand. Sitting in the front passenger seat, Roger turned to check on the old man. And he wasn't looking good. His forehead was shiny with perspiration, and his breathing labored. "How are you feeling, Father?"

"Are we stopping soon? I'm feeling nauseous."

"I'm sorry, Father, but our orders are to go as far as Brive-la-Gaillard, where they expect us. We can pull over for a few minutes if you wish, but otherwise, we need to keep going."

The priest scowled; these damn trips, it was always the same thing, covering hundreds of kilometers only to end up in the same situation as before. It was one version of the story of his life.

# # #

The owners of the house in Brive—a solidly built spacious stone structure sitting off a secondary road, surrounded by a wooded area—were not much younger than the priest. They welcomed him warmly and showed the three men to their rooms. A copious dinner had been prepared; tomato soup, a leg of lamb with a two-bean side dish, and then a hunk of *beaufort* and green grapes. The old priest barely touched the food while JP and Roger wolfed the meal down. Small recompense for their labors, but you had to take what you could get. The hosts asked about the trip, inquired about the priest's health, and studiously avoided discussing the circumstances that caused him to be a guest at their dinner table.

In the morning, after a leisurely breakfast, Roger said they needed to be off and thanked the couple for their hospitality. Some two and a half hours later, they arrived at their destination in a small town in the southwest, where the priest was again given a warm welcome.

As he settled into his room—it had a small balcony overlooking a charming square—he smiled for the first time since that unfortunate encounter two nights ago. He was safe here in the countryside, in a town like so many others. Let Bruno Edremal—the boy's full name had come to him during the drive—knock himself out running around Lyon; he would never find him here.

CHAPTER ONE

April 2011
Marseille

NOTHING HAD CHANGED. THE ROOM the size of a broom closet, the pigeons whirling in the air shaft, the windowsill stained with their droppings. He tried to make sense of the papers on the desk before him, but he couldn't even focus on the words, let alone decipher their meaning.

Jacques Mornnais. Stealing his money had only sharpened his desire to kill him. But he wasn't the only one. There were the painters, Li and Wen, the maid Ella (even if she was back in the Philippines), and, of course, Father Paul. He wanted to kill them all, but every time he tried to think *how he* would do it and who would be first, the pounding in his head started up, the pain so intense he couldn't see straight.

"How's it going, Bruno?" A muscular man with square shoulders stuck his bald pate—it was the color of dark honey—into the doorway; there wasn't enough room for the two men in the tiny space. The speaker was Charles Paoli, one of Sauveur's cousins. He'd driven in from La Ciotat to help Sauveur's law partners sort through his files. Charles Paoli wore a well-fitting grey suit with white pinstripes; he had a crisp white pocket square, his pink shirt open at the collar to reveal a gold chain around his neck. Charles

Paoli's voice burst the bubble of confusion, and Bruno replied in his normal voice; it was low, the suggestion of violence ever present, no matter the words he used.

"Slowly, it's taking me some time to put it all together."

Charles Paoli nodded; he was not intimidated by Bruno, not by his voice, not by the man himself. And he moved on to the real reason for his presence today: "Your old boss, Jacques Mornnais, do you have any idea where he may be hiding out these days?"

Bruno turned around in his chair to face Charles Paoli and looked at him with his empty eyes: "Jacques? Not a clue. And you, I don't suppose you have any ideas?"

"I'm afraid not, my friend. Well, it's been great seeing you again, Bruno. Thanks for helping out and take care."

# # #

Bruno heard Charles Paoli talking with Sauveur's partners; trying to make out what they were saying, he pushed his demons back into their hiding place. But their voices were too low, and he returned his focus to the mass of documents before him. He remembered working on the deal with Sauveur. It had involved acquiring a building using a strawman to avoid any hint of a conflict of interests — in this case, the strawman was a woman — with the idea of subsequently transferring the property to someone else. Bruno decided that he'd see to it that the straw woman kept the property. He had his reasons, and the thought of screwing the other person brought a smirk to his lips. He arranged the documents in the file, brought them to the partners, and explained all that they needed to know about the transaction.

He left the office and walked down Rue Saint-Jacques, thinking about Charles Paoli's question. *Merde,* if only he *knew* Jacques' whereabouts. And then the thought of Jacques once again brought images of the painters, the maid, and the priest to the fore. Their faces coalesced into the now familiar feeling of vengeance, and he felt a wave of anger erupt like hot lava coating his body. They had all wronged him, and he would not stop until he exacted his revenge.

But where to begin? Back in Lyon, the mirror in Chez Michel had awakened childhood memories of Toulouse, and without thinking, he'd told Michel that he was going to that city. The vision of Toulouse arose now, reawakening his grievances. His only hope was that being in Toulouse would dissipate the angry fog in his brain and show him the path to avenge the harm that had been done to him. He had nothing to lose.

# # #

Charles Paoli walked down Rue Saint-Jacques and headed to the Vieux Port, where he was meeting friends for lunch. Was Bruno telling the truth when he said he didn't know Jacques' whereabouts? The man had worked for Jacques for twelve years, and then Bruno had mysteriously turned up first in Lyon and then in Marseille, where Sauveur had taken him on. But had Jacques gotten in touch with him? He wished he knew the answer to that question.

In fact, Charles Paoli knew Jacques' whereabouts; he wanted to see him punished, but he'd been warned off taking matters into his own hands. For now. But when the government stopped protecting Jacques, he needed to be ready to act, and it would be helpful to know whether Bruno would be helping his old boss. All he could do was to try to keep tabs on Bruno for as long as he was at the law firm.

CHAPTER TWO

RICHARD HAD LEFT NEUILLY A few days ago, and now Alex and Eugene were driving down to Trubenne to join him there. A cloudy weekday in early spring, with traffic light on the A6 motorway. Alex recalled the last time she'd travelled down this road, back in January 2010. Marie-Agnès Duvalois had been mugged in the Paris metro and she and Mag suspected that Jacques Mornnais was behind the attack. To escape his wrath, Alex drove Mag to Trubenne where she stayed with Charlotte. Charlotte. Collateral damage when Jacques' hired assassins killed Sauveur Paoli. Which brought her thoughts around to Jacques Mornnais.

"I'm so relieved that Jacques has disappeared; at least he's not looking for me! It feels great not to worry about him any longer."

"Yeah, I imagine that you're the least of his problems right now. Although there are others who are not so happy that he's gone missing."

"Like whom?"

"My bosses at the Bureau, for one. They were glad to get his files, but that is the past, and they were looking to build a future relationship. And then, of course, there's our friend Bruno. Helped himself to a shitload of money that Jacques had stashed at the château, but I don't think that made him happy; come to think of it, I don't think Bruno's capable of being happy—the man has got a pretty narrow emotional range. I'd say it goes from a slow boil to a volcanic eruption. Anger in one form or the other. What I'm trying to say is he liked taking the cash, but it was secondary. What he was really looking for was to confront Jacques."

"Confront him?"

"I guess I should say 'kill him.' That would probably be a more accurate assessment of his state of mind."

"And what *is* Bruno's state of mind?"

"Good question. Let's see. He's an intelligent man, but prone to violence. Is he a sociopath? Maybe. And then, there's the problem with his amnesia. Try to imagine what it's like to have lost your memory and then to recover it in bits and pieces. And wonder if you can even know what you don't know? Unknown unknowns and known unknowns. It must be frustrating, the not knowing. If I had to pick one word to describe his state of mind, I'd say it's a mess."

"And after all the time you spent with him, he didn't tell you anything helpful about Jacques."

"Not really, except that he knew where to find and access Jacques' secret hiding place in the château. You know, I never would have found Jacques' files had it not been for Bruno! And I wonder if there isn't some clue to Jacques' whereabouts hidden in his subconscious. But I said goodbye to him in Dijon, and I doubt that our paths will cross again."

"I hope not."

They picked up the A7 motorway outside of Lyon. As they headed towards Nîmes, the clouds dissipated and Alex realized how attached she had become to the Provençal countryside, with its lush vegetation and clear blue skies. How happy she was to be returning to Trubenne, leaving Jacques Mornnais and Bruno Edremal behind for good.

CHAPTER THREE

Paris

VITAL VESLA DE TRUBENNE WAS on his way out when he saw his wife standing motionless in front of the bay window in the living room. He hadn't seen her for two days—they had separate bedrooms and led separate lives.

"Well, I'm off to the office," he said, although she hadn't asked where he was going. She turned to face him:

"I think I'll be going for a run, now that the bloody rain has stopped."

"Be careful not to slip and fall, you don't want to break your wrist again."

Her thin lips cracked a smile, "No, I'll take care. If not, I'm sure you'll find someone to sue."

He wondered for a moment why she ran almost every day. She had the gaunt face of a professional cyclist, and if her figure was trim, it was too thin for his taste—he liked to put his hands around something more than skin and bones. Yet the intensive exercise didn't seem to make her happier. What *would* make her happy? Then he remembered that Anne's *raison d'être* was to be dissatisfied. She argued with shopkeepers, fought with her few friends, only their cat found unconditional favor in her eyes.

They lived in an elegant art deco building in Paris' sixteenth arrondissement. But the public areas needed freshening, and, should he prevail on the co-owners to approve the expense, he was sure that Anne would complain about that too.

By the time he had walked through the lobby to the waiting taxi he had forgotten Anne; he had much more important business on his mind.

# # #

La Belle Fermière was already crowded when Vital arrived. Lawyers, politicians, businesspeople, those on the way up and those on the way down, all stopped by to breakfast on the restaurant's legendary fried eggs, the whites firm but not rubbery, the yolks a perfect balance between solid and liquid.

An American lawyer, Merv Peters, had held court at the restaurant almost every morning. His colleagues still talked about his spectacular accident. After dinner at Chez Blondie, a trendy *bouchon* in Lyon, he'd driven his car off a winding road, rolling down a hillside. The vehicle had caught fire, but Merv had died instantly of a broken neck. They gossiped about his estate. Some said he had left an art collection worth millions. He'd never married, and a sister in the United States had inherited the artwork and his two homes, one in Paris and one in the countryside in Normandy.

Vital remembered Merv. It seemed like many of the wealthy expatriate Americans—and there were plenty of them not only in Paris but all over France—had gone to him for advice. He gave the impression of being someone's wise uncle, and if the tales about his art collection were true, he had made a lot of money. Vital wondered how Merv did it, being a sole practitioner. Then he smiled, for Vital had his own system, which was the reason he would be leaving for his midday appointment after he stopped by his office to read the morning's mail.

# # #

Babs Thomason had hired a new girl to help serve lunch, who was now shuffling around the kitchen, trying to look busy. There was nothing for Babs to do until the guests arrived, but that didn't prevent her from walking back and forth from the living room to the kitchen and back again. Babs knew that this behavior was useless, but she was no more able to stay out of the kitchen than she was to stop examining herself in the intricately carved Lemon Giltwood mirror that hung in the living room.

The mirror threw back the Image of a *dame d'une certaine age,* her face recently tightened and smoothed. Gone were the lines and under-eye pouches; gone too was any expression, just a bland expanse of skin. But that was what she had wanted, and she was pleased with the result. She had traded her *faux Chanel* tweed suit for a more relaxed look: a plunging V-neck sweater and trousers. This was the style adopted by the President's wife. A former movie star, she still looked svelte in her skin-tight pants. The same could not be said for Babs.

But Babs could be excused for being nervous. Since the disappearance of Jacques Mornnais, who had regularly used her apartment for private meetings, her income from that activity had fallen off. Today Vital Vesla de Trubenne was coming for another discreet lunch, and she wanted everything to be perfect.

Babs had known Chloe, the late wife of Vital's uncle Richard. The Vesla de Trubennes were an old Protestant family, with a lineage dating back to the early Middle Ages, a coat of arms, and what Chloe had described as a crumbling château in the Languedoc region. Babs hoped that having Vital as a client might bring her closer to French aristocratic circles. But until now, no such luck. In fact, Babs suspected that Vital did his best to avoid her, unless she could be useful to him on occasions such as this.

The doorbell rang, and Babs tore herself away from the mirror. Vital was at the door, and she suppressed a small twitch of disappointment; he had arrived early, removing any opportunity for small talk with his guest. Air kisses were exchanged.

"You're looking well dear lady." Babs basked in the compliment—it was so easy to flatter her.

"Thank you, you're too kind, really," and she ushered him into the living room. She spotted a dot of dandruff on the shoulder of his dark, well-cut suit, and reflected that Jacques Mornnais ought to have patronized his tailor—instead, he had seemed to wear his shapeless, off-the-rack suits like a badge of pride. Vital's guest was late, and he had to suffer through the agony of making small talk with Babs while they awaited his arrival.

CHAPTER FOUR

SOMETIMES, EVEN WHEN YOU CHECK all the boxes, things go south. Take Antoine Tipette. Not quite handsome, but good-looking, nonetheless. Not a genius but bright enough: he excelled in mathematics, necessary to succeed in the French school system. He had sailed through his studies, landed a job with a French consulting firm that specialized in mergers and acquisitions in the hi-tech sector, and he was moving slowly but surely up the ladder. All good, you say? But during his studies, he'd discovered cocaine. In the beginning, he'd do a line or two at parties, over the weekend. But then, as the pressure at his job increased, he turned to coke to help him pull all-nighters, and soon the context of his use moved from recreational to professional. One box came unchecked when he'd been stopped while driving erratically and the blood test revealed his drug consumption. A friend who'd been In similar circumstances gave him the name of the lawyer who had made everything disappear. "He's excellent," said his friend, "But it's gonna cost you, big time."

# # #

Antoine had gone to Vital's office on Avenue Kléber for their first meeting. When he told Vital whom he worked for, the lawyer questioned him closely about his current project. Antoine told him that he was working on a proposed merger of two companies that built offshore wind farms. But now he was worried that the stupid arrest might impact his reputation, or worse.

"I can understand that you wouldn't want to lose your job," Vital said, "That deal between Wind Power Unlimited and Mondial Matrix sounds fascinating. How far along are the negotiations?"

"I really shouldn't be talking about this at all, but yeah, things are coming along."

Vital had the same aquiline nose as Richard Vesla de Trubenne and his niece Alexia, but whereas they were tall and slender, he was short and squat, and his dark brown eyes showed that he was missing the gene for blue eyes as well. He removed his glasses — they had heavy black frames — placed them on his desk and sighed.

"This won't be easy, you know, but as it's a first offense, I think we can have the charges dropped. But I'll expect your complete cooperation."

"Of course," said Antoine, "Whatever you want me to do."

"I'll need to talk to some people. Then we'll have to see each other again. But rather than you coming to my office, I know a woman who makes her apartment available for private meetings. It's so much more intimate and relaxed."

Is he hitting on me, or what, thought Antoine.

"Her place is on Rue Lalo. It's not too far from here." Vital ripped a sheet of paper off a pad, wrote Babs's name and address and pushed the paper across his desk. "I'll let you know the day and time after I've made some inquiries."

When Antoine told him about the meeting, his friend laughed.

"Don't worry," he said, "it's not sex he's after, just money. You'll find out soon enough."

# # #

When Antoine met Vital for lunch at Babs's apartment, things became clearer. As they helped themselves from a large seafood platter, the lawyer explained:

"Your situation is a bit more complicated than I first thought. It seems that the police want to crack down on people driving while under the influence of drugs. However, I've been able to call in some favors that are owed to me, so I still think that, in the end, the charges will be dropped. But you may remember that I told you that I'd expect your cooperation." He slurped an oyster, savoring the meaty texture and smell of the sea.

"Uh, sure, what do you have in mind?"

"I'd like to know more about the merger between Wind Power Unlimited and Mondial Matix. WPU is a company I've been following for some time now, and of course anything that touches them is of interest to me."

Àntoine had been peeling a jumbo shrimp. He'd started with knife and fork, but frustrated by his slow progress, he was picking the thin covering off with his fingers. As he heard Vital, he snapped the head off and looked up: "You're asking me for confidential information, I can't do that."

"Not really. I'm sure I could find a lot of the information from analysts' reports that are in the public domain, but it's just that I'm swamped, I don't have the time to read through all that stuff, so you'd just be giving me a summary of what is available anyway."

Now Antoine understood what his friend meant when he said: "It's gonna cost you, big-time."

# # #

Antoine and Vital met a few more times at Babs's apartment. As Antoine filled him in on the status of the negotiations, Vital slowly amassed shares of Wind Power Unlimited: if the merger went through, their price could double overnight.

Today Antoine arrived only a few minutes after Vital. There was no need to go through the charade of Antoine merely sharing public access news. True to his word, Vital had had the drug-related charges dropped, and Antoine "cooperated" accordingly.

"This is probably the last time we'll meet," he announced. Vital fixed him with a quizzical stare: "Oh?"

"Yeah, it looks like the deal will be signed in the coming weeks, and the firm is sending me to Gaillac, where WPU is located. There's a pile of work yet to be done."

"So, it's going through?"

"Looks that way, but I'll call you once the papers are signed."

"Make sure that you do, I've got a lot invested in WPU."

The morning's brilliant sunshine had faded away, the sky resuming its colorless gray mantle. Antoine sniffled, and Vital wondered if he was snorting coke every day, or whether it was merely the effect of the damp weather.

Babs's girl cleared away the plates and served a *sauté de veau Marengo*, courtesy of a local caterer. Afterward, Babs herself brought out dishes of warm *Tarte Tatin* and coffee. She had not served wine. Vital only drank sparkling water during the day, and he was sure that Antoine would be much better off *sans vin.* The meeting over, Antoine left first.

"I trust you're satisfied with everything?" Babs asked Vital.

"Oh yes, quite." He handed her an envelope.

She thanked him and asked, "Will we see you again?"

He stiffened momentarily, as if she'd ventured onto forbidden territory, before replying, "Not for the moment, but not to worry, I'll call you when the need arises."

She walked him to the elevator and smiled. "Perhaps *à bientôt,* then."

The door closed shut. As he rode the elevator to the street, Vital thought of his mother: *Il faut séparer le bon grain et l'ivraie* (one must separate the wheat from the chaff) she might have said. *Maybe I ought to find another place for my confidential meetings.*

# # #

Babs walked back into the dining room. A marble-topped commode stood in front of one of the windows. She had placed a blue and gold cloisonné bowl on the commode and filled the bowl with an artistic arrangement of apples, pears and grapes.

During lunch, Babs had been careful not to hover over the men, remaining in the kitchen at the other end of her apartment. But now that the dining room was empty, she walked over to the commode and removed the cell phone that had nestled in the fruit bowl. Babs had changed the fruit for each visit, but her technique remained the same.

The recordings were inaudible in places, but Babs had understood enough of the conversations to realize that an opportunity had presented itself. Perhaps not the ideal opportunity—she would have preferred to meet a wealthy widower, a man old enough to be taken with her new face. But she made the best of the situation: she called her broker that afternoon and placed an order for more shares of Wind Power Unlimited.

CHAPTER FIVE

Le Marais, Paris

THE APARTMENT ON RUE DE Turenne was a mirror image of its inhabitant, Antoine Tipette. The address in the Marais suggested a hip lifestyle, but inside, the rooms were small and dark, and the odor of his beloved Golden Retriever, Ollie Blue, was omnipresent.

Keeping a large dog in a small apartment made little sense, but Ollie Blue was the repository of whatever capacity Antoine possessed for love, for warmth, for affection. All that remained was an almost negligent disregard for others, except as they might help further his career.

Antoine coaxed Ollie Blue out of his apartment and into a waiting minivan. They drove to a kennel in Neuilly that was run by a group of veterinarians who had state-of-the-art facilities for keeping pets. It was expensive, but nothing was too good for Ollie Blue.

Night had fallen by the time he returned to his apartment. He would be spending the next few weeks in Gaillac, outside of Toulouse. He'd never been to Gaillac, but it sounded like a shithole town with nothing to do but work. On the other hand, he'd heard that Toulouse had an intense clubbing culture—he hoped so. Packing was not difficult; he was used to traveling.

Antoine crawled into bed, but instead of sleep, he relived his luncheon meeting earlier in the day. The lawyer had convinced himself that the merger would go through, and he'd been buying up shares of WPU stock. The share price had been rising on rumors of the deal, but in fact it wasn't a sure thing. If things went south, he'd have to let Vital know in time for him to unload his shares. The money-grubbing lawyer wouldn't take kindly to losing his bet on the merger, and Antoine didn't want to get left holding the bag if the share price took a dive.

If only he hadn't been pulled over by that dumb cop. Everyone did coke, his co-workers, even his boss for fuck's sake. It was such a big deal about nothing. Perhaps it would do him good to get away from both Vital and the smell in his apartment.

CHAPTER SIX

Rue des Arts, Toulouse

BY THE TIME SHE REACHED the second-floor landing, Jacqueline Fitzgerald was out of breath. How she wished that they had bought an apartment in a building with an elevator. At first, they had found the steep, winding stairway, with its tiled steps and oak trim, charming. But that was before she had to drag groceries home, before her husband had left her.

She dropped the groceries in the entry, headed for the living room and collapsed into the one armchair that was not strewn with clothing. Jacqueline sat, unseeing, wondering for the umpteenth time, how it had all come to this. She wasn't really looking for an answer, and none came. After a few minutes, she roused herself, brought the groceries into the kitchen and put them away.

The apartment was spacious. One hundred and fifty square meters in the historic center of Toulouse, it was one of the things that had attracted them. But with space comes obligation: floors to be mopped and vacuumed, endless surfaces to be dusted and polished, a long balcony crowded with plants and small shrubs to be watered.

She sighed: she seemed to be doing a lot of sighing since her husband had walked out on her. At the sink, she filled an empty Evian bottle and started to water the small forest outside the windows. Working her way along the balcony, she nipped dead leaves, went back and forth to the kitchen to refill the water bottle.

Rue des Arts was a narrow street, fronted by the red brick buildings Toulouse was famous for. It was easy to peer into the apartments across the street. There were no curtains on the windows, just indoor shutters that were only closed when the inhabitants went to bed.

A motorcycle rumbled past, the noise from its exhaust reverberating off the canyon of facades. A taxi pulled up and stopped in front of the building opposite hers, and a thirty-something man got out. His hair was fashionably unkempt, and he wore an expensive leather jacket. She looked up from watering to watch as the driver unloaded his suitcase from the trunk. The man paid him, fiddled with the key to the front door, and entered the building. Some minutes later she saw the passenger open the shutters in two rooms that overlooked the street, directly across from her balcony. Even now, she had a love of fashion, and the well-cut leather jacket caught her eye. She wondered briefly who he was, what he did, and then went back to her task.

She didn't care about the balcony anymore, but she had put the apartment up for sale, and she felt that the greenery would enhance its value. One more refill and the chore would be completed. More noise wafted up from the street, and she saw that another taxi had stopped under her windows, blocking traffic. This time, the drivers of the cars behind the cab were leaning on their horns. She'd noticed how belligerent and aggressive motorists in the south seemed to be, and it only added to her feeling of depression.

She watched as the taxi passenger alighted. Unlike his predecessor, this man was older and much more substantial. She imagined that he had been a rugby player; Toulouse was, after all, in the heart of rugby country. And although he had a large frame, his movements were light and precise. He too entered the building across the street. Curious, she scanned the windows, waiting to see where the new arrival lived. But after a few minutes had gone by, she concluded that either his flat was at the back of the building, or that he preferred darkened rooms. Perhaps he had a point there.

The images of the new neighbors dissolved, and Jacqueline set about straightening up the living room, readying it for another assault of sneakers and outwear when her children returned from school later in the day.

CHAPTER SEVEN

Paris

CANAL SAINT-MARTIN. PATRICK TRABERT sat on a bench on Quai de Valmy. It had rained that morning, but the clouds had blown away, leaving a pale blue sky. The air was still damp, and the sun's rays felt good on his face. He stared at the traffic that moved past—barges, a tour boat, a police motor launch—and replayed the conversation with Véronique this morning.

"It's now been almost four months since we agreed that you would leave, and you're still here."

"I know, but I haven't found work, and you don't expect me to sleep on the street, do you?"

As he asked the question, he suspected that wouldn't bother her very much. His gaze moved across to the other side of the canal, where a small city of brightly colored tents was perched at the water's edge. Perhaps he'd join the thousands of homeless that lived wherever they could find a place to pitch a tent or erect a rudimentary shelter: the Bois de Boulogne, the Bois de Vincennes, on grassy patches along the ring road—the possibilities were as unappetizing as they were numerous. If he went back to Marseille, David would insist on his paying the rent up-front, and he was down to his last euros. He could feel the tears of depression and self-pity welling up, and he tried to force them back.

Patrick reached in his jacket pocket, feeling the coins and a small roll of twenty-euro bills, all that remained between him and destitution. *Fuck it* he said to himself and started to walk to the McDonalds on Rue Faubourg du Temple to enjoy one of his last meals. As he reached his destination, the minute hand on the clock of destiny moved, his phone rang, and the caller made him an offer he couldn't refuse.

# # #

Over the years, Emma and Max Martolla had done very well, buying property in and around Aigues-Mortes, fixing it up and selling it. They had both left school after *collège,* the equivalent of junior high school, but that had not prevented them from flipping properties and turning a profit. They had been in love when they married, but they grew apart as their fortunes flourished. Emma bought a large house inside the city's ramparts, and Max found refuge in a sprawling *mas* in the *Parc natural régional de la Camargue*. Their story should have ended there, each financially secure, each going their own way. But well into late middle age, refusing to admit that his achievements were due as much to luck as to skill, Max gave in to the urge to do something else: open a sushi restaurant. He called it Citadel Sushi, and he convinced Emma to join him in the adventure.

Patrick had worked at the restaurant last year until Max lost his temper one day and fired everyone. He reversed course a short time later, but by then, Patrick had already left to return to Marseille, where he'd met Véronique.

# # #

Emma was on the phone. "Patrick," she gushed, "how are you?"

"Doing just great, Emma, and you?"

"Patrick, I know things didn't work out as you'd hoped when you were here, but a lot has changed since you left. Filippo our chef—you remember him—has come back."

How could I forget the fucker, it's because of him that Max fired us all.

"Yeah, I remember him."

"Well, Patrick, I'm the one running Citadel Sushi now, Max is ill and spends his days at the *mas*. We're preparing for the tourist season, and I was wondering if you could be free to come back to work here through the summer. Then we could see what happens after that."

"Uh, I dunno. I'm pretty tied up right now."

She continued: "And I have a small studio where you could live, so you'd have no rent to pay. What do you say?"

"Well, it sounds interesting. You say Max won't be there?"

"That's correct, he's retired now." That was perhaps stretching the truth a bit; Max continued to show up periodically to terrorize the staff, but perhaps Emma felt there was no point in going down that road.

"Well, I need to think about it. Can I call you back?"

He went into McDonalds, stood in line, ordered a double cheeseburger, large order of fries and a chocolate shake. As he ate, Patrick considered his other options: they went from bad (living with Véronique) to very bad (living rough). He waited an hour, called Emma back to say that he'd be able to free himself up and when did she want him to start.

He dreaded the last call that he had to make, but it was unavoidable.

# # #

Phuket, Thailand

Caroline Trabert had just settled into bed when her phone rang. She looked at the clock on her night table: who could be calling her at eleven p.m.? Certainly not any of her friends here in Phuket. She felt a pain in her abdomen, and her breath came in shallow spurts as she looked at the caller ID. *Patrick.* Of course.

"Hi Mom, how are you?"

"Patrick, what is it? Do you know what time it is here?"

"Sorry, Mom."

Caroline was silent.

"Mom, are you there?"

"Yes, Patrick. I'm here and wondering why you're calling at eleven o'clock at night. While I have a pretty good idea, why don't you tell me?"

"The good news is that I have a job. They've offered me back my old job at Citadel Sushi. And Emma's going to put me up in one of her studios."

"And the not so good news?"

"C'mon Mom, I just need a small loan to pay for my train ticket and to tide me over until I get paid."

Caroline closed her eyes. *Would it never end? Would Patrick never get it together?* His last job had been with an internet bank, but then, he'd been fired when they outsourced. *He's a bright boy, well educated. Why can't he do something better than cooking rice?*

"Mom?"

"Patrick, I will wire you 500 Euros. Do not ask for more and do not ask again." Caroline had started to speak calmly, but as she continued, her voice rose to a shriek before she ended the call, "This.is.the.last.time." A few deep breaths to calm her thumping heart, and a vow to stand firm the next time he called. Whether he knew it or not, he'd gone to the well for the very last time.

As it turned out, cutting the umbilical cord was not that simple.

CHAPTER EIGHT

Rue des Arts, Toulouse

EVER SINCE HE'D SEEN THE mirror at Chez Michel, Bruno's dreams took up all the space in his head while he slept. Dreams of darkened rooms, of blurred outlines and shadowy figures, dreams of rosy facades, of towers, the sound of church bells pealing. They filled him with terror. In one dream, a door opened, and he saw himself as a child. He was in Toulouse, that much he knew, but what was he doing there? He tried to look inside, but the door closed, and he woke up, his heart thumping as he gasped for breath.

Most of his recollections had been wiped away when he was submerged in the river Arroux. But now, memories had slowly begun to return. Was it due to talking with Eugene, the American? Maybe, but the green and red lights of memory had also flashed when walking the streets of Lyon, where he had grown up, and Marseille, where he had worked. Would other memories surface when he wandered through Toulouse? Bruno was afraid of what he'd discover, yet he had no choice: he had to plunge into the black holes and uncover the unknowns.

It didn't take him long to unpack, and he hurried outside to explore the neighborhood. He turned on to Rue Croix Baragnon. At the end of the street stood the Saint Etienne cathedral, with its stained glass rose window.

Bruno wasn't interested in architecture, and the mixture of Romanesque and Gothic styles meant nothing to him. On the other hand, his eyes were drawn to the tall brick tower at the rear of the cathedral.

Shops, bars, and restaurants lined the edge of Place Saint-Etienne, dwarfed by the giant religious edifice. It was a balmy spring day. He managed to find an empty table, ordered an espresso and sat staring at the tower, waiting for an image or a thought to appear. But none did, and after a while, he got up and meandered down Rue Fermat. The antique shops reminded him of the art dealer, Nicolas Pagès. Pagès had done the paperwork for a stolen painting that he'd hoped to sell, but then the art dealer had disappeared, and Bruno didn't know what had happened to the picture. All he knew was that Nicolas had turned up dead. He pushed the thought to the back of his mind—it had nothing to do with the reason he was in Toulouse.

At the end of Rue Fermat, he came to Place Sainte-Scarbes, and even Bruno was not immune to the charm of the square, with its elegant Italianate facades. *Just the sort of place where Jacques would have lived.* The thought of Jacques Mornnais—it was harder to push away—stayed with him as he turned on to Rue Ninau. He felt irritated now. The historic center was so perfect, almost too beautiful, and it made him think that he was walking on the set of a movie.

Suddenly, he forgot about Jacques Mornnais. Across the narrow street was a long, ancient brick wall. There was an entrance with a carved fronton, but the massive wooden doors were shut tight. This was the first time he'd walked down Rue Ninau, and yet he was sure he'd seen that wall before; had it been in one of his dreams? *Servientes Mundi* read the brass plaque affixed beside the door. Bruno tried to remember his schoolboy Latin: didn't it mean "serving the world," or something like that? Were these the offices of a courier service, a firm of consultants, or some charitable organization? He'd come back another day, earlier this time. When the doors were open, he might learn why there was something familiar about the wall.

Bruno continued to walk along a street that skirted Le Grand Rond, a spacious park. The odor of Asian cooking grew stronger as he approached a stand that sold Vietnamese food. He hadn't eaten all day and ordered some fried noodles with chicken. The food reminded him of the Chinese painters and the Filipina maid, Ella. And then Jacques. The American had said that Ella was back in the Philippines, he had no idea where the painters might be, and it looked as if Jacques had disappeared, just like Father Paul. Jacques had attempted to kill him, as had the painters and the maid. But his body and soul had remained intact. It was Father Paul who had harmed his body and destroyed his soul; given a choice, he'd go after Father Paul first. But as things stood, he'd have to take what he could get.

CHAPTER NINE

Museum Le Louvre, Richelieu Wing

LI XIO WAS SITTING ON a bench in Room 13 of the Richelieu Wing when a sudden chill crept up his back. Shivering badly, he stopped copying the images of infants in the painting before him and looked around to see where the blast of cold air was coming from. But all that Li saw were two women whispering softly to each other, and they didn't seem cold at all. It wasn't the first time that this had happened; at random moments, he'd shudder as if caught in an icy wind, and then the wind would dissipate, leaving him with nothing more than the memory of intense cold. But he knew there was no point in looking for the source of the frozen air, for the cold originated within himself each time he remembered throwing the hated man, Bruno Edremal, into the river Arroux.

The painting, sometimes called The Little Bacchanal, was by the 17th-century artist Nicolas Poussin. Li was more than a little familiar with Poussin's work. When he'd worked for Jacques Mornnais, he'd enjoyed doing Poussin forgeries; he'd even created his own Poussin-inspired painting—*Baby Moses in the River*. Of course, Jacques would take the paintings away as soon as they were completed, and recently, Li started to feel the urge to do a painting in the style of Poussin for himself. Thus, he found himself in Room 13, studying a scene from the infancy of Bacchus, the god of wine.

He started sketching again, recording elements he'd incorporate into his painting: the infant Bacchus drinking from a bowl into which grape juice had been squeezed; the adult men and women; two infants embracing each other…Li visualized a clearing in the forest where little Bacchus, surrounded by lusty infants, would be drinking from a bowl held by one of the men. But in place of a tree in the background he envisioned a satyr. The mythological scene, as he imagined it, was disconnected from any legend. But that didn't matter to Li; he had his own story.

The memory of Bruno Edremal slipped to the back of his mind as his slender fingers moved the pencil across the page. He could hardly wait to return home and start work on his project.

CHAPTER TEN

Rue des Arts, Toulouse

ANTOINE HAD TO ADMIT THAT his temporary lodgings were much nicer than his apartment on Rue de Turenne. Light streamed in as he opened the shutters on the two windows overlooking Rue des Arts. The place smelled fresh and clean, the hardwood floors were waxed to a soft glow, and there was room, plenty of room. *Too bad I can't live in a place like this in Paris.* But it was an impossible trade-off: limited light and space in exchange for his hectic Paris social life.

Across the street, he saw an extended balcony, filled with small shrubs and plants in flower. A tired-looking woman was poking around the greenery. She looked up for a moment, lowered her head and went back to work. *There's not much privacy here* he realized and thought that he ought to buy some sort of tree to place outside his windows. But for now, he'd have to remember to close his shutters at night.

It didn't take him long to unpack, and he thought it best to sort out the paperwork for his car rental today. Walking up the street, he felt adrift, disconnected. Whenever he traveled, Antoine was always glad to return home to the Marais. He missed the familiarity of his surroundings, and most of all, he missed Ollie Blue. Here in Toulouse, there were the usual boutiques, but everything seemed so small, so lacking in the energy that he felt in Paris. As he approached the car rental agency, he passed a shiny black door; above it was a large gold and black neon sign marked *Shangri-la.* His spirits lifted: a club right up the street, open from 11p.m. to 7 a.m. He'd give himself a day or two to settle in, take the pulse of what was expected from him at Gaillac, and then he'd check out the *Shangri-la*.

CHAPTER ELEVEN

Rue des Arts, Toulouse

WHEN SHE AWOKE THAT MORNING, Jacqueline Fitzgerald put on the same black turtleneck sweater and the same pair of jeans that she'd been wearing all week. She had a closet full of beautiful clothing—she'd been a personal shopper in another life—but she took the path of least resistance and grabbed the garments draped over the back of a chair in her bedroom. Her chestnut hair hung around her shoulders in a lifeless mass, thin lines had begun to make their way from her nostrils to the corners of her mouth. She'd gotten used to people saying that she was beautiful, but that was then, and now she avoided examining her face too closely in the mirror.

Her therapist had counseled her to avoid sitting around the apartment all day—she ought to be going out, seeing friends, taking walks around the beautiful city. But Jackie had no friends, and she hated Toulouse. She had walked up to a nearby newsstand and bought the *International Herald Tribune*, which she now sat reading in her living room. With luck, that would take up the morning, and after lunch, she'd shop for groceries at the Carmes market and then wait for the boys to return from school, start preparing dinner, look at television, and go to sleep. And begin all over again the next day.

She felt a surge of anger as she read about the continuing "birther" controversy in the United States. What a vile man Donald Trump was: another racist who couldn't stomach a black man in the White House. Those thoughts brought back memories of her life in Washington D.C. before Josh had been promoted and transferred to Toulouse. She had had friends there, a job that she loved, an independent income. And now, aside from a monthly check from Josh, nothing. A small light flickered at the back of her mind and grew brighter. Perhaps she did have a friend here in France. Well, maybe not a friend, exactly, but someone she knew from back home: Alexia Thornhill.

Alexia had been a stylist, and on occasion, their paths had crossed. She remembered Alex: tall, slender—perhaps too slender—blonde, with an aquiline nose and piercing blue eyes. An intense woman, friendly but in a superficial way. Jackie had the impression that Alex's job occupied her to the exclusion of all else. She'd heard that Alex had discovered her husband in her bed with another woman. There had been a divorce, and the rumor was that Alex had moved to France.

So, they had something in common. Where was Alex living, she wondered. Probably in Paris, far from out-of-the-way Toulouse, with its noise and its rugby mania. Wherever Alex was, Jackie was sure that she would be too busy to come for a visit, but following her therapist's advice before second thoughts could intrude, she sent Alex an email: how about coming to Toulouse for a visit?

CHAPTER TWELVE

Trubenne

ALEXIA THORNHILL STOOD IN THE shower, immobile, soothed by the hot water running down her back. When she had worked in Washington, her morning shower, like her breakfast, was an obstacle to be overcome in the rush to get to work. But here at Trubenne, their château on the outskirts of the eponymous village, other rhythms had taken over. Alex gently massaged a red scar on her shoulder, reliving, as she did every morning, the terrifying afternoon on Sauveur Paoli's boat. Henchmen sent by Jacques Mornnais had killed Sauveur and Charlotte, and Alex had been wounded in the assault. Shortly after that Jacques Mornnais had disappeared—killed or abducted, one couldn't be sure. "But let's say he's still alive," Eugene had said, "I'm sure he has more pressing concerns than to continue to look for you. So, there's little danger in you returning to Trubenne."

Aside from Marie-Agnès Duvalois, her cousin Charlotte had been her only friend here in France. Now, there was only Marie-Agnès, but she was busy running her restaurant in Lyon. And of course, Eugene. It was true that they'd become much closer since she'd been shot. He'd started to tell her about his past, but she felt that talking to Eugene was like peeling an onion with an infinite number of layers: with each revelation came another set of unanswered questions. She wasn't sure that you could ever know someone entirely, and perhaps those shadowy corners were part of his charm.

She turned the water temperature dial from hot to cold, shivered in the jolt of the icy spray, jumped out of the shower and wrapped herself in a large bath sheet. They didn't have a clothes dryer at Trubenne; the laundry was hung to dry outside, and the towel was rough, reddening her skin as she rubbed herself dry. Alex opened the window to let the cloud of steamy air escape and stepped into the much colder hallway. In her bedroom, she pulled on a jacquard knit sweater, a fresh pair of well-fitting jeans and low boots. She might be living in the country, but that was no reason to neglect her appearance.

CHAPTER THIRTEEN

Aigues-Mortes

PATRICK AND VÉRONIQUE HAD NOT seen much of each other over the past few months. They had organized their time so that when one of them was at Véronique's apartment in Paris, the other was at her house in Fontainebleau. Yet, there was something perverse in their relationship. Véronique nagged him about leaving, yet she would invite him down to the house when she didn't want to be alone. Or she'd ask him to accompany her when meeting with clients as she sold off her late father's inventory of furniture and *objets d'art*. He said he wanted to leave, and yet he didn't make much of an effort to find a job that would provide him with financial independence. So, on the day that Patrick left for Aigues-Mortes, they promised each other that they would stay in touch.

He enjoyed the train ride south. For once, he had paid for his fare and was not in constant fear that a conductor would come by to check his ticket. Emma had offered to pick him up at the Nîmes train station; Montpellier was closer to Aigues-Mortes, but he would have had to change trains at Nîmes. *She must really need me if she's so nice*—after the events of the past year, he was a lot less trusting and more on his guard—*We'll see what happens.*

They stopped by the restaurant, and Patrick ate dinner with the rest of the staff. Filippo, the chef, greeted him with a cold smile. If there was clearly a lot less tension, now that Max was no longer there, Patrick was still not at ease.

"He's really not around anymore?" he asked Filippo.

"Nope, he's got some kind of illness, and he usually stays out at his *mas*, leaves us in peace."

"And how is business?" Patrick sought to reassure himself that there would be work for him in the coming months.

"Not to worry my friend, there's plenty of business for those that keep their eyes open and their mouths shut."

Patrick didn't have the opportunity to ask him what he meant, as the wait staff crowded into their seats to eat before the evening shift. Later, Emma drove him to his lodgings. An old bicycle leaned against the side of the building: "That's for you, you'll need it to get around."

The studio was cold and damp. Spring may have come according to the calendar, but even in the south, April nights could be chilly. He undressed and slid under the plump down comforter and waited to warm up. Sleep did not come quickly—it was still difficult for him to put Bruno and Eugene Stokes out of his mind. He hoped never to see either of them again. Just thinking about the muscular Frenchman sent shivers up his spine. As for the American, he frightened him as well, for Patrick could not see what lurked behind his smooth façade. Well, at least they were now firmly in the past. As he felt his eyes growing heavy, Patrick remembered Filippo's last remark and his final thought was that he'd try to avoid the chef as much as he could.

CHAPTER FOURTEEN

Gaillac

FOR SOME, GAILLAC WOULD BE worth visiting. The site of battles in the Hundred Years War, it had also suffered the butchery of the French wars of religion, and it's great, rose-colored abbey could trace its origins to the late tenth century. The Celts and after them the Romans had cultivated wine along the banks of the Tarn river; today the wines of Gaillac bore the coveted *Appellation d'origine controlée* label.

But the history of Gaillac was of no interest to Antoine. He had been afraid to carry his supply of drugs with him on the plane, and the focus of his thoughts was on where he might find a reliable source of cocaine, for he now relied on the drug to get him through the day. He drove into the city center before he realized that WPU's headquarters were in an industrial park on Gaillac's outskirts. The area fell short of being an eyesore, but that wasn't for lack of trying: low-lying, prefab buildings, a few scrawny trees, rows of parking spaces. He felt a brief wave of gratitude that he was housed in Toulouse and not expected to live out here.

He was given a small office, a cubbyhole really; even when he'd first started consulting, he'd had better work conditions. His bosses were due down soon, but for now, he was on his own. As he set about reviewing documents and interviewing management, he could feel the hostility, sense the tension. *No use trying to hide things. If there's something amiss, I'll find it.* For a moment, he thought of Vital, who had invested heavily in WPU. *I've got to remember to let him know how things are going.* By six p.m., the place had emptied out, but Antoine worked on. When he looked up at the office clock, he saw that it was almost eleven p.m. — it was time to call it a day.

On the drive back, to cheer himself up, he thought about Ollie Blue and imagined that his dog would be waiting for him when he returned to his apartment. He'd call the vet tomorrow to make sure that he was okay. On the way into Toulouse, he stopped at an all-night grocery, bought some frozen meals, wine, and water. The long day had been exhausting—he didn't relish working for the next weeks in WPU's fraught atmosphere—but he couldn't fall asleep. Then he realized that his shutters were open, letting the light from the streetlamps pour into his bedroom. He got up, stood at the window for a moment, looking across the street. Everyone must be asleep: the shutters were closed. It was the only way to have some fucking privacy. After dinner tomorrow, he'd go up the street to the *Shangri-la* and try to score some coke to help him get through this assignment.

CHAPTER FIFTEEN

Paris

VITAL TOOK THE METRO TO Place de la Concorde. It was quicker — and a lot cheaper — than taking a taxi, and there was no point in throwing money around. He stopped to gaze at a display of men's accessories in the window of a shop that sold a bit of everything. He thought that he recognized a pair of socks that his client Antoine Tipette had worn to one of their meetings; they were a shade of burgundy with a tiny white pattern. A few minutes later he emerged from the shop with the same pair in gray, shoved the package into his briefcase and went next door to the Club des Deux Continents.

He felt at ease in the C2C, where one did not risk running into people who were, well, not like us. For example, there was Michel de Clermont d'Auvergne, from a lineage that was as old as his. He had wanted to talk to Michel, but casually, and seeing him seated there, he seized the opportunity.

They embraced, discussed the country's recent legislation that banned full-face veils: something needed to be done to protect French civilization. They moved on to consider the upcoming marriage of Prince William and Kate Middleton: it was a pity that France did not have a constitutional monarchy to provide some colorful entertainment, rather like bread and circuses. Vital then asked about Michel's father; he had heard that he was not well.

"Thanks for asking. He's doing as well as can be expected, I guess. And how is your uncle, Richard? Now, there's a hardy specimen!"

It was the perfect opening. "Of course, physically, Richard's in great shape for a man of his age. But I fear that he's slipping a bit up here," pointing to his head.

"Oh, really?"

"Yes, he can be quite forgetful, off in his own world. We were wondering if living in that big apartment with only a maid isn't too much for him."

"Oh, I wouldn't worry about Richard, if I were you. I saw him not so long ago, and he seemed just fine to me."

Vital felt a vibrating in his pocket. C2C had a rule that no cell phones were allowed in the reception rooms; they marred the relaxed atmosphere. He glanced at the caller ID as the phone continued to vibrate. It was Antoine.

"I'm afraid I must take this call. Please excuse me," he said and stepped out into the hallway.

"Well, what is it that's so important?" he snapped at Antoine.

"I thought you should know, I'm not sure if the deal is going through. Maybe yes, maybe not. You might want to think about unloading your shares while the market is still up."

"Not yet. Just keep me posted. *Qui ne risque rien n'a rien.* No risk no reward."

Vital went back to the salon. The conversation with Michel hadn't gone the way he hoped; there was no point in wasting any more time.

"It was great running into you, let's get together one of these days."

"Yes, of course." Michel's mouth puckered as though he'd eaten a sour apple, the rotting fruit of an ancient tree.

# # #

Babs was having second thoughts, in fact, third and fourth and fifth thoughts. Wind Power Unlimited's share price rose, dipped a bit before rising again. It had been doing that all week. She had never understood the stock market and decided to call an old family friend to ask his advice.

"Do you know anything about this company, my dear?"

"Not really, just some information that a friend shared with me. They may be merging with another company. Or not."

"I see. And this friend, have you asked them about the fluctuation?"

"Um, they're not available right now."

"Yes, I can see why that might be disturbing to you, not knowing what's going on. May I ask, would you come out ahead if you sold your holdings right now?"

"Ye…yes, but I'd only make a small profit, not what I'd earn if the merger went through."

"And if it does not go through? Then you'd probably lose quite a bit, would you not?"

"Ye… yes," she repeated. She had more than an inkling of what he would say next.

"If I may, my dear lady, I would advise you to sell immediately. I know that's what your father would have told you. The stock market is not for amateur players, and if you cannot afford to take a loss, then get out while you still can."

Babs had a sixth thought, called her broker and placed an order to sell.

CHAPTER SIXTEEN

May 2011
Rue des Arts, Toulouse

SHE CLEARED THE KITCHEN TABLE, rinsed the plates, sticky with Nutella, and placed them in the dishwasher. A glass, half full of milk, slipped from her hand and shattered on the tile floor. In her bare feet, she tiptoed to avoid the shards that glittered in the morning sunlight. A twinge, and drops of bright red blood mixed with the sparkly glass. *Oh fuck. Another start to a great day.* Jackie overcame the urge to hurl the remaining dishes onto the floor; instead, she went into the bathroom to bandage her foot.

I've got to get out of here, a little voice screamed in her head. She hobbled down the stairs, bought her newspaper, found a seat at an outdoor café and started to enjoy the coffee, the sunshine, and the blue sky, until she remembered what a shit day it was and went back to feeling sorry for herself. But the universe, it would seem, was determined to give her a break. Back in her apartment, she left the mess in the kitchen and opened her email. Where she found a message from Alex: she was living in the Languedoc region in a tiny hamlet called Trubenne, not that far from Toulouse, and she'd love to come for a visit, how about towards the end of the month?

Jackie felt the weight of loneliness lift from her shoulders. Her midsection, gripped in a tight vise, relaxed, and her breath came more easily. Buoyed by those few words on her computer screen, she set about cleaning the mess in the kitchen.

CHAPTER SEVENTEEN

Rue des Arts, Toulouse

MID-MORNING. THE FIRST THING BRUNO felt when he opened his eyes was fatigue. He'd been dreaming, but trying to remember his dreams exhausted him. He felt ill at ease in Toulouse. The city was so noisy, wherever you were, you'd run into throngs of students and millennials. There was a club up the road called the *Shangri-la*: that made him laugh. Late at night, the partygoers shouted and argued outside his building. The noise crept up from the street, bounced off the walls, slipped through the cracks and woke him up. He guessed that the revelers had come from the club. After a few minutes, they would move on, but he tossed and turned for hours before sleep came.

He knew he had come to Toulouse for a reason; there was a connection to the city, but he couldn't figure out what it was. Perhaps, if he returned to Rue Ninau, it would come to him. When he'd been in Lyon and Marseille, he'd returned to familiar places, and some memories had returned, starting in his dreams and then melting into his waking hours. It had worked in those two cities, so why not here?

Most of his memories were uncomfortable, but he needed to find them to become whole again—no, to become whole for the first time.

# # #

This time the massive oak doors were open. A neo-classical private mansion, built by an industrialist in the eighteenth century, overlooked a cobblestone courtyard, crowded with cars and a minibus. Bruno hesitated—there was a café on the corner across the street—and went to sit outside and watch the comings and goings before deciding his next steps. Some men were loading camping equipment—tents and sleeping bags—into the minibus. His heartbeat quickened when he saw a group of children exit the building, accompanied by two priests in long black robes. They got into the van and drove past him. Bruno had a sudden vision: he was in the van, seated next to Father Paul, the priest's hand resting on his shoulder. He shut his eyes, willing the vision to continue, but the image faded. No matter: the images of Father Paul and Toulouse had merged into a single thought: Father Paul was the reason he'd come to Toulouse.

Jacques, the maid, and the painters slipped deep into his mind, Father Paul now taking up all the space. Toulouse was not the only place the old priest had assaulted him—far from it—but Bruno couldn't escape the feeling that it was here that he'd catch up with him. When he did, he'd give full rein to his desire for vengeance. As he sat on the café terrace, Bruno began to think about the form his revenge would take.

CHAPTER EIGHTEEN

Toulouse

BRUNO, ON EDGE, PACED BACK and forth in his apartment. He shivered as he remembered the years at the *Centre d'Etudes Saint-Bernard,* remembered, as well, the time they visited Saint Stephen's Cathedral, the priest's hand on his back sliding down to caress his buttocks. And then back at their house…Saint Stephen's Cathedral, it was right around the corner; he'd go over there and ask about a priest named Father Paul. He hated being in Toulouse, surrounded by noisy students and drug-addled clubbers. But he wouldn't let up until he found Father Paul and made him suffer as he had suffered. Where was the old priest hiding? He felt that the answer lurked just beyond his consciousness, hidden from view. Irritated by the unknown unknowns, he decided to go out for a walk, when his phone rang.

A man he knew from Marseille was calling to say hello. They'd heard he was in Toulouse, and how was Bruno doing? Oh, keeping busy. We were wondering would you have the time to do us a favor?

"Depends, but sure, why not?"

The man described what they had in mind, and added, "Thanks, appreciate it. We'll call you when we're ready. Terrible what happened to Sauveur, wasn't it?"

"Yeah, but you know, whatever goes around comes around, it's just a question of time."

He was glad to hear from the people in Marseille, working for them would give him something to do while he waited for a sign that Father Paul was in Toulouse.

# # #

A perfect spring day, the rose bricks glowing in the warmth of a sapphire blue sky. Bruno rose early, bought a copy of *L'Equipe*, and sat on the terrace of a café on Place Saint-Etienne in the shadow of Saint Stephen's Cathedral. It was an unusual edifice, built in two styles of Gothic architecture, one tall and one rounded. *It's lopsided,* he thought, *like everything else about the church,* and ordered an espresso.

Nearby, a woman with faded auburn hair was aimlessly stirring a large cup of *café au lait* as she read her newspaper. He didn't find her attractive—he had preferred young Asian women—but he noticed her hands as she folded and refolded the pages of her *International Herald Tribune*. Her hands: the fingers were long and graceful, elegant even, despite the short, colorless nails. They reminded him of Marie-Agnès Duvalois, the one they had called the red-haired cow; she had beautiful hands as well. The image of Marie-Agnès briefly reawakened thoughts of Jacques Mornnais, but the image of the black-robed priest pushed those thoughts away, and the question that now preoccupied him again came center stage: *is Father Paul in Toulouse? And if he is, how can I find him?* Bruno scowled, ordered another espresso, and tried to interest himself in the results of the French Champions League matches. However, with thoughts of Father Paul swirling through his head, he found it difficult to focus on the printed page before him.

# # #

Jacqueline Fitzgerald had finished her coffee. It was time to do the day's food shopping. Today she would go to the Victor Hugo market. The place had thrilled her when they first came to Toulouse. First, there were the regional specialties: duck, sausage, cheese. And then, all the rest: pastries, bread, meat, fowl, fish, pork, fresh fruit and vegetables, prepared food. In the beginning, the market was beautiful and exciting, overflowing with gastronomic delights. Later, when her life began to head south, she found the crowds claustrophobic and the sellers' banter—she had previously taken it as a sign of authenticity—irritating. In a fleeting moment of self-awareness, it occurred to her that it was not the circumstances that created her moods, but rather that her moods were like a film projected onto the screen of her circumstances.

With her market trolley in tow as she left the café, Jackie walked past the man engrossed in *L'Equipe*. A momentary feeling of recognition: *do I know him*, she wondered. But that was not possible: she knew no one in Toulouse.

CHAPTER NINETEEN

BRUNO HAD YET TO GO inside Saint Stephen's Cathedral. Yesterday, when he'd walked up to the dark brown doors, something stopped him from going inside. It was the same dread that had come over him after spending a few minutes in Father Paul's room at the *Centre d'Etudes.* But today would be different, he told himself. His contacts from Marseille were expecting his help today, but he'd go to the cathedral to ask about Father Paul before heading to his meeting.

Bruno crossed Place Saint-Etienne. Next to the cathedral stood the stately Préfecture, its sidewalk still littered with bottles from last night's partying. *Fucking assholes* he muttered, forgetting the many bottles he had emptied in his years as an alcoholic. He entered the cathedral. Immediately, childhood memories of feeling insignificant and powerless under the high, vaulted ceilings and the stained-glass windows returned. Only a thin light filtered through the windows, bathing the cathedral in a brown glaze.

Bruno walked down the long aisle of empty pews until he caught sight of a priest in a side chapel. He felt his heart racing as he approached the altar.

"Excuse me, Father, I'm looking for Father Paul, I believe he is one of the priests here."

"Father Paul? I'm afraid you are mistaken; there's no priest by that name in this cathedral, my son." It was the voice the priests used to chastise the boys, and he felt humiliated by the sound of it and the way the man's beady eyes peered out at him through his glasses.

Humiliation, joined by frustration, turned into anger as he strode rapidly out of the dark cathedral into brilliant sunlight. The contrast further infuriated him; he picked up one of the empty bottles that littered the sidewalk, and his arm, unbidden but with a mind of its own, prepared to hurl it against the cathedral walls. But he had work to do this morning, and he replaced the bottle where he'd found it and continued on his way.

# # #

Bruno was early for his meeting. He walked down Rue Ninau, hoping that the sight of the building that housed *Servientes Mundi* would awaken other memories, but his mind remained blank. He passed the Vietnamese food stand, but today, the aroma brought back no memories either. His mind was on the task before him as he strode up Allée Paul Sabatier.

A dark green ribbon, bordered by graceful trees, charming villages and scenic countryside, starts near Bordeaux and unwinds as it flows through Toulouse and on to Sête. From there it continues, passing close to Aigues-Mortes before emptying into the Rhône at Beaucaire. On the section of the ribbon that stretches from Toulouse to Sête, is the Canal du Midi, a marvel of seventeenth-century engineering.

At the top of the Allée, Bruno came to the canal. This time, his memories returned. At the sight of the canal's waters, he again saw himself crawling out of the river Arroux, shivering as he dragged his body up the muddy riverbank. The maid. The painters. Jacques. He would deal with them later. Eyes squeezed shut, he focused now on how to find Father Paul. He replayed his encounter at the cathedral; the priests never changed, did they? Always cold and arrogant. A thought arose: he'd teach that fucking priest a lesson. Another thought: the church had hidden Father Paul too well; it would be impossible to find him. Maybe he should just forget about revenge, about punishment. He'd finish the job for his friends and then return to Marseille. Bruno felt the sour taste of bile in his mouth as he was pulled in two directions: stay in Toulouse and continue his search or give up and return to Marseille.

On the opposite side of the canal, Bruno entered a neighborhood called Côte Pavé. He walked past elegant residences and rows of *Toulousaines,* the one- or two-story houses typical of that part of the city. The chic area gave way to more prosaic low-income apartment buildings with pale gray facades, small balconies, and white metallic shutters. He continued to Rue Sergent-Vigné, walking past number 17. It was a quiet street, the only noise coming from the faulty exhaust of a motorbike that drove past. The rider was the terrorist, Mohamed Merah; he would be killed in a shootout with the police less than a year later, but today Bruno paid no attention to him. A few minutes later the van he was waiting for pulled up in front of number 17. The driver got out, and together they opened the doors at the back. Along with the pallet of rice a motorcycle and a bike were attached to the sides of the van. "All good?" asked Bruno.

"Yeah, no problem," said the young man as he removed the bike from the van. He rode off towards the Mirail housing projects, and Bruno got behind the wheel.

An hour later he exited the A68 motorway at the medieval village of Castelnau-de-Montmiral. Next to him on the seat was a scrap of paper with directions to a farm. He remembered when he and Tarek had done pick-ups and deliveries for Jacques—it could have been a pair of chalices, a painting, an antique commode, whatever. Back then, Tarek had done the driving, and he mostly slept. But unlike the trips with Tarek, this van had no GPS, and now it was up to him to figure out where the fuck he was going. Country roads—they were the same whether you were in Brittany or Occitania: deserted, narrow, the pavement cracked by the elements. *Not the place to break down* he thought, at the same time as the farm came into view.

CHAPTER TWENTY

A FIGURE IN TATTERED BLUE overalls was standing in the yard. He wore a dirty white undershirt, and a wrinkled cap of the same faded blue color was pulled down on his forehead. A cigarette hung from his lower lip; the long ash fell as he motioned to Bruno to drive the van into a hangar.

Bruno noticed a door in the hangar's wall. He had a good idea of what was behind that door, but knowing for sure was not part of his job. They unloaded the pallet, and Bruno wheeled the motorcycle out of the van. He handed the van's keys to the man, "Here, these are for you. I'll be off now, if there's nothing else."

Bruno's errand completed, a red wave of anger trailed behind him as he rode back the way he had come. Anger at what the priest had done to him—the dip in the river Arroux had juggled those memories free. Frustration, too; his inquiries at Saint-Stephen's had led nowhere, and no new ideas of where he could look for the old priest had come to him. Lost in his thoughts, he missed the turn-off for Castelnau-de-Montmiral and instead found himself heading north toward Gaillac. He felt hungry—it had been hours since he'd left the café on Place Saint-Etienne—and he decided to stop in Gaillac to grab a bite.

The majestic abbey church, Eglise Saint-Michel, came into view as he crossed the Tarn River. The church had seen much turmoil since its establishment as a Benedictine abbey near the end of the tenth century. Many of its buildings had been destroyed by religious wars, disease, and revolutions. Today, culture and spirituality existed side-by-side: the abbey was also home to a wine museum and a tourist office.

Bruno felt drawn to the Abbey; he parked his bike nearby and walked inside. He took no notice of the wine museum but found himself on a terrace overlooking the river. A feeling of unease came over him, and he walked back out to the street. It was then that he saw a black-robed figure exit the abbey. A troop of small boys, like a school of fish, followed in his wake. For a moment, Bruno was in that group, then the image of the children faded, but this time the priest remained: a living, frail old man.

Bruno felt the familiar pounding behind his eyes. His recollection of their retreat in Toulouse was vivid as he relived being touched and penetrated by the priest. The horrors of Lyon had continued here.

But was it possible that the black-robed figure was Father Paul? He remembered the delivery truck driver in the café in Lyon; he'd said the consignment was headed to the southwest, but that was a pretty big area.

The priest entered one of the houses that stood on Place Saint-Michel. The *Résidence Saint-Michel* was an ancient building; its rose brick façade was faded with age. Bruno rang the bell and a young priest, whose neck was covered by an angry case of adult acne, opened the door.

"May I help you?"

Fear coursed through Bruno's body and his mind went blank. He couldn't think of anything to say.

"No, that's okay."

He turned on his heel and walked back to his motorcycle. As he approached the bike, something made him turn to look at the old house. A black-robed figure had stepped onto the small first-floor balcony, surveying the small square in front of the church. The brilliant sunshine glinted off his glasses, and a soft breeze moved the folds of his robe. When the priest saw the man looking up at the house, he quickly stepped back inside, but not before Bruno saw him. But what exactly had he seen, he asked himself? A figure in a black robe with indistinct features. Was the church hiding Father Paul in the *Résidence*, or was the black-robed figure merely another old priest? *Before he started to make his plans, he needed to be sure that the figure he'd seen was Father Paul. And that meant returning to Gaillac.*

# # #

Father Paul collapsed on the bed. He wheezed, his breath making a whistling sound, and although the room was comfortable, his forehead glistened with sweat. Who was the stranger on the motorcycle? The man was too far away for him to get a good look at his face; could he have been Bruno Edremal or one of the other boys? How had they found him? He shivered as he recalled Bruno coming to Saint-Bernard a few months ago. The man's voice had been cold with anger. It had sounded like a low growl coming from the pit of his stomach. And those eyes, had he seen fear in them as well, the same fear he had sensed in the boy? *Let him stay afraid and stay away.*

The wheezing died down. Father Paul sat up, his eyes focused on a point in the past, got up, and walked across the room to the corner where some of his belongings had been placed. There was the trunk that the delivery company had transported from Lyon, and next to it, a beaten-up black wheelie bag made of canvas. He pulled the bag over to the bed, spun the dials on the lock, and the bag popped open. He slowly removed the contents on top—files of correspondence, magazines from the diocese—until he reached the other magazines he'd hidden there. A quick step to make sure that the door to his room was locked. Then he removed one of the issues and slowly leafed through it, stopping at the page he was looking for. He leaned back on the bed, eyes empty, staring at the ceiling, all the air sucked out of his body. Afterward, he stood up, replaced the contents in the bag, and locked it.

Father Paul tried to collect his thoughts; perhaps he'd overreacted, and the man was nothing more than one of the many tourists who passed through Gaillac. Only a few knew of his presence here, and they kept that knowledge to themselves. As for himself, he would avoid the balcony during daylight hours just to be safe.

CHAPTER TWENTY-ONE

Vitry-sur-Seine

OVERCOME BY THE MONOTONY OF hauling produce and filling bins, by the drudgery of replenishing shelves with an infinite variety of jars and tins, Li couldn't wait for his shift at the supermarket to end. When it did, two thoughts fought for attention as he punched out: how he ached all over and how eager he was to return home to work on his paintings.

Back at his apartment, he dealt first with his body; his soul would have to wait. Stretched out on his bed, he scanned his body and breathed into the pain. He started with his fingers before moving on to his hands and then up his arms; with a deep inhalation, the breath came down to his toes, moving from his feet to his calves, then his knees, his lower back, and his shoulders. All that bending and lifting, it was fine for those in their twenties, but he was twice their age, and he felt the difference.

Once he had relaxed his muscles, he made a pot of tea, put the supermarket out of his mind, and his thoughts turned to his passion. Li was working on a series of paintings inspired by the time he'd spent at the Château d'Hélène, and as he contemplated the paintings he had completed, he felt a warm wave of pleasure roll through his body. His most recent effort—a work in progress—stood on an easel. A wood warbler perched on the branch of a tree, its green and yellow form seemed to tremble with excitement, the painting capturing the tension before the bird flew into the sky. But today, rather than finishing his tableau, Li turned to his pet project: creating his version of a story featuring the infant Bacchus, done in the style of Nicolas Poussin.

He spread his preliminary sketches on the table and continued to flesh out the composition of the painting as he had imagined it: a joyous, bucolic scene with laughing infants and doting adults surrounding the lusty infant Bacchus.

Memories from his childhood arose and then dissolved like wisps of smoke. Another set of memories: his years as a student, learning his craft, then the voyage to France and the prison that was the atelier at Château d'Hélène. He frowned, chased those last thoughts away, and returned to his story of the infant Bacchus. Li worked until his stomach rumbled; reluctantly, he put aside his work, made dinner, and crawled into bed, lulled to sleep by his vision of the painting.

CHAPTER TWENTY-TWO

Phuket, Thailand

EVENING. THE SKY HAD OPENED up just as Caroline Trabert reached her favorite bar. She went there most days after work, chatted with the bartenders and whoever happened to be seated near her. She was deeply tanned, her skin the color of a turkey that had stayed too long in the oven; deep lines were etched around her eyes and her mouth. But she didn't mind, or maybe she didn't notice. She was happy here in the tropics, far from the back office of Alpine Trading Bank, with a more than adequate nest egg to pay for anything she could possibly want. Except that Caroline had also been paying for something she did not desire: the debt-ridden lifestyle of her grown son.

Lost in thought, she sipped her drink and ruminated. She felt frustrated and even depressed that Patrick was unable to support himself, no matter what he tried. And now he was back to working in the kitchen of some sushi restaurant. Would it never end? Was this the best he could do? When he had called her for another "loan," she had told him this was absolutely the last time, and she intended to hold firm.

An Asian man at the table next to hers was nursing his drink. Smiling, he turned to her: "What a downpour, the monsoon season is upon us."

Caroline took in the broad, pockmarked face, the enlarged pores. His skin was shiny, as though molded out of wax. He wore a pale beige linen suit, a gold chain around his neck and a Rolex on his wrist.

"Yes," she agreed, "It's quite impressive. Are you from Phuket?"

"I'm here on business," he said, not really answering her question. "And you?"

"Oh, I work in a bookshop here, I'm a long way from home."

"I assume you are French?"

"Indeed."

"And your family, are they here with you?"

"Uh, no, there's just my son, and he's back in France."

"Ah, you must miss him, so far away."

Not really. What I miss is having a son who is self-sufficient. "Of course I do. But he needs to work, you know, I cannot support him forever." She had not meant to talk about Patrick with a total stranger, but what difference did it make, she'd probably never see the man again.

"Yes, we hear about unemployment in France. Pardon my asking, but does your son have a job? I ask because you said you could not support him forever."

Caroline felt relieved; she would be able to present Patrick in a more favorable light. "Actually, he's just starting a new job; he'll be managing a sushi restaurant in the south of France." It was a small exaggeration, but it made her feel much better.

The man sipped his drink, studied the ice cubes, before speaking. "How interesting, I'm a rice exporter, perhaps I could have one of my associates contact him?"

"Oh, I don't know." *What would happen when they discovered that he was washing pots and cooking rice?*

"What does he have to lose? We might be able to make him an interesting proposal."

What the hell, she decided. *Maybe there will be something in it for Patrick. Let him deal with it.*

She wrote Patrick's name and phone number on a napkin. "Here it is, Mr…?"

"Oh, pardon me. Just call me Joe."

"Well, yes, Joe, I guess you never know."

"It was nice talking with you," he said as he stood up. He was on the short side, his jacket resting on a large belly, a complement to his round face. Caroline thought he was quite unattractive. She would not have wanted to sleep with him, but she was disappointed that he hadn't tried.

CHAPTER TWENTY-THREE

Paris

HE LIKED TO START HIS promenade at Place Blanche, strolling past the sex shops and stores selling cheap clothing. He'd start on the south side of Boulevard de Clichy, go as far as Barbès-Rochechouart, cross to the north side of the street, and retrace his steps back to Place Blanche. Vital Vesla de Trubenne never went into any of the shops that he owned; it was enough for him to see that they were open for business. There was no danger that he'd be seen by anyone from his milieu. Still, once his promenade was finished, he hurried to jump into a taxi and return to his office.

As he did each day, Vital checked the price movement of WPU's shares. The share price was volatile—the spikes were followed by drops. It looked like some investors preferred to take short-term gains, rather than patiently wait for the merger to be announced. Or not. He had bought his shares when the price was low, and if he sold now, he'd make a comfortable profit, but not the killing he expected should the merger go through. Vital hadn't heard from Antoine since the consultant had called him at his club, and he wondered how things were going at Gaillac. Why hadn't that little shit contacted him to let him know whether the deal was on or off? No, he told himself, all is well. Don't lose your nerve now. If there were a problem, surely he would have heard from Antoine. Unlike Babs, he decided to sit tight.

# # #

Gaillac

A final round of negotiations had started on Thursday morning. New information on WPU's projected revenues had come in. The numbers were crunched yet again, new Memoranda of Understanding were drafted, and the discussions continued. The hours of endless meetings stoked Antoine's smoldering irritation—they were just wasting time. That night, the team was lodged in an inexpensive hotel nearby, and he managed to score some coke with a lawyer from WPU. Come Friday morning he was in less than stellar form, and he felt worse still when things started to fall apart in the afternoon. During a pause for coffee, he followed the Wind Power company lawyer into the bathroom, where they snorted a few more lines. He felt better now, participated with renewed energy in the increasingly acrimonious negotiations. By evening, the deal was off, and he had come down from his high.

Over the past two days, Antoine had forgotten about Vital. Driving on the secondary road that led to the highway, he suddenly remembered the lawyer and his obligation to him. Antoine pulled off onto a gravel shoulder and tried to reach Vital, but his call would not go through. *Fucking countryside*, he drove a little further and tried again. The connection was weak, but Vital's voice mail picked up. The line crackled as Antoine started to leave a message, "It's me, it's all gone south. You'll see on Monday", when the line dropped. He tried to call back, but this time he had no luck. Never mind, he'd call Vital back when he arrived home.

At first, Antoine thought he was hallucinating when he saw the tractors lined up on the highway. As he got closer, he understood that his eyes were not deceiving him: farmers, protesting low prices for their produce, had blocked the road, leaving a single slow-moving lane for automobile traffic. His heart raced, his breath was shallow. The day's heat sat heavy in the car. The AC system had stopped working. *Shit.* He felt so hot that he opened the car window, but the fumes from the tractors made him nauseous. It was late by the time he had reached Toulouse and parked his car. Antoine knew what he needed to do: go to the *Shangri-la.* As for Vital, he'd left the guy a message, and he didn't want to hear him whining that the deal had gone south. Back in his apartment, he showered, dressed in his casual clubbing attire and walked up the street; he'd score some more coke, and celebrate the end to the painful last few days.

# # #

Vital had been checking his voicemail, waves of anxiety rising each time there was no message from Antoine. Then he saw Antoine's name; he listened, and his breathing became shallow as the static on the line crackled, garbling the words. Vital pushed the replay button, and this time he managed to hear the message: "It's me, it's all done."

Relief mixed with unease; Vital wanted to know all the details, the backstory. He called Antoine that night, but the consultant had started on his drug-infused weekend and could not be reached.

CHAPTER TWENTY-FOUR

Rue des Arts, Toulouse

FRIDAY NIGHT. BY THE TIME she had finished cleaning the kitchen, it was almost midnight. Jackie started to watch *Shutter Island*, dozed off midway through the film, awoke with a start, turned off the television, went into her bedroom and immediately fell asleep. And, as had happened for the past weeks, she was wide-awake at four a.m., her heart racing. Sleep eluded her. Jackie walked into the living room, stood at the windows and looked down at the empty street. Were any of her neighbors awake, she wondered. Almost all the shutters were closed, and she saw no lights in any of the windows.

Noise shattered the calm of Rue des Arts. Footsteps, laughter, and loud voices—the commotion was moving towards her building. Two men came into view. Thirty-somethings she would have guessed, pushing garbage bins along the sidewalk, shouting and laughing some more. A jacket caught her eye when they came to a halt opposite her building. Jackie stared at the supple leather, the color of coffee with just a splash of milk, the light from the streetlamps reflected in the soft folds across the back. She had started to open her window to say something to them, ask them to be quiet, when the man in the leather jacket turned around and looked up: "Why don't you get back into bed, you old whore?"

She froze as both men giggled and made obscene gestures. Frustration and unhappiness burst out in a scream, "And why don't you shut the fuck up", before she shut her window and stepped back into the darkness of her apartment.

Eyes squeezed shut, body trembling, she tasted the salty tears that ran down her cheeks, worried that the noise had disturbed her children. But all was suddenly still. The two men must have parted company, for the man in the leather jacket now stood in front of the door to the building across the street, fumbling in his pockets. Too upset to return to bed, Jackie sat on the sofa facing the window, waiting for her breathing to return to normal. As she did so, the lights went on in the apartment that faced hers. An arm, encased in soft brown leather, was closing the shutters. *Shit, that asshole lives right here; I'm sure that's the man I saw getting out of a taxi a few days ago.*

# # #

Antoine had slept in for most of the day on Saturday. At midnight, he did a line of coke and got ready to head out to the *Shangri-la.* He'd seen that Vital Vesla had been trying to reach him, but hey, it was the weekend, and he'd already left the guy a message, so he put Vital out of his mind and looked forward to another night of booze and drugs as he took off for the club.

CHAPTER TWENTY-FIVE

Seeing the old priest in Gaillac had unsettled Bruno. He knew he had to return to Gaillac, but what would he do when he got there? He had the feeling of being weighed down, and at the same time, stretched thin. The remnants of a frozen meal landed in the garbage can; he had no appetite. All he could do was gulp down some Badoit to settle his stomach. The sun had set; perhaps if he got some sleep, he'd find the way forward. And a dream came, almost as soon as his head hit the pillow.

He is walking down a canyon-like street, lined with boutiques, but when he tries to enter a shop, he discovers that the door is locked. Further down the street, he sees a building with a monumental entrance, and behind it, the answer he is looking for. His pace quickens, he hears his footsteps echoing off the tall buildings, and the sound of metal scraping against the cobblestones. Noise fills the street now; the massive door is fading, and he hurries to reach it before it disappears altogether. He tried to remain asleep to finish his dream, but the insistent ringing of the downstairs door buzzer jarred him awake. *What the fuck?* It didn't take Bruno long to pull on his jeans and run down the stairs. He opened the front door, came face to face with Antoine: "Hey man, thanks for letting me in, I can't seem to find my keys."

Silence. Bruno, still partly in his aborted dream, stood rooted in place, blocking Antoine's passage. With one hand, he grabbed Antoine's throat.

"You woke me up, you little fucker. The next time, I'm going to kill you."

Antoine's mind went blank. What was he doing here, why was the huge man choking him? How could he have awoken him, he'd been walking down the street? Better not to argue, the guy was hurting him.

"I won't. I promise. I'm sorry. Won't happen again, man. Really," he croaked.

Bruno followed Antoine up the stairway and watched as he reached under the doormat for the extra keys he kept hidden there. He continued up to his apartment on the third floor, at the back of the building. All Bruno wanted was to return to his bed, conjure up the wooden door, and continue his dream. But he was wide-awake until dawn, and when he finally drifted into unconsciousness, the door had disappeared.

CHAPTER TWENTY-SIX

Aigues-Mortes

WHEN PATRICK SAW HIS MOTHER'S caller ID, he was puzzled. Since money was their only topic of conversation, why was she calling? After their last call, he was sure that his mother wouldn't be offering to send additional funds, so he let the phone ring. When she tried an hour later, and again after that, he began to worry, and on her third try, he answered.

"Hi Mom."

"Patrick, I've been trying to reach you."

"Well, I've been busy."

"Yes, I can see that. Anyhow, I'm glad you answered, I have some news for you."

"Yes?" *She can't be coming back to France, so what could it be?*

"I met a man…"

"Um, that's nice," he interrupted, wishing her to get to the point. He'd been playing a video game, and he wanted to get back to it.

"A man who could help you."

"Oh really, and how's that?"

Caroline related her conversation with Joe. She omitted to tell Patrick that she had enhanced his job description; he'd have to work that out when the time came.

"So, one of his associates will be calling you. Patrick, this could be an opportunity for you to make some money, so try not to screw it up."

"Thanks for your vote of confidence, Mom."

"I'm trying to help you, Patrick," and with that, she began to complain about his lack of success, his sucking money from her like a vampire.

"A vampire: do you think that's an appropriate metaphor for your son?" he interrupted her.

"What did you say?"

"Nothing Mom, listen, thanks, really, but I've got to run. Bye."

Caroline went back to the bar where she had met Joe. She thought she might run into him there again; she'd be able to tell him that Patrick was expecting to hear from his associate. But Joe was long since gone, and Caroline had to content herself with a gin and tonic. Or two.

# # #

A week later Patrick was meeting Joe's colleague Maurice—just call me Momo—in the shade of the plane trees on Place Saint-Louis in Aigues-Mortes. At first, Patrick liked Momo—he had warm, dark brown eyes and a ready smile. He didn't seem to mind when Patrick pointed out that he was not the restaurant's manager; his job was to make rice and wash pots.

"I see. Look, Patrick, here's all you have to do. The restaurant will be receiving a shipment of rice. Under no circumstances should you unpack the shipment; just call me, and I'll send someone to pick it up. If anyone asks, you just say that it looks like there was a mistake and you're returning the shipment to the sender. Do you think you can do that?"

"Yeah, sure."

"So, when the person comes to pick up the shipment, he'll give you an envelope with your commission. Does five hundred euros sound fair for making a one-minute phone call?"

"Yeah, very fair, Momo."

"You've hardly eaten anything, you're not sick or something, are you?" Patrick had been cutting his pizza into small pieces, pushing them into a circle at the center of his plate.

"No, just not hungry."

"Well, I've gotta run," said Momo. He threw a 50-euro note on the table. "I'll send you a text message with the number you need to call. Just do as I said, no fuck ups, you'll be great."

Patrick watched Momo's back disappear into the crowded square. Once he was gone from sight, Patrick asked himself if their conversation had indeed taken place, then berated himself for having agreed so readily to Momo's offer. Patrick hadn't bothered to ask why the shipment should not be opened: he figured he knew the answer. Out of nowhere, he thought of Véronique. What would she have done? He felt that he knew that answer as well: she would never get involved with a guy like Momo. That was fine for Véronique. Her father had bought her an apartment and a car, he'd supported her, and now she was making money by selling off the gallery's inventory. When he reflected on the unfairness of it all, he knew that he'd done the right thing.

CHAPTER TWENTY-SEVEN

Trubenne

EARLY MORNING, THE AIR STILL fresh, the sky already springtime bright. Richard and Eugene were seated at the long table in the kitchen, studying the proposal from the vineyard consultant, pouring over the map he had provided.

Alex was packing her bag. She would leave later today to visit Jackie. She wouldn't be staying long—just two days—but long enough to have a break from the pastoral rhythms of life at Trubenne. A few days in a city, feeling the pavement under her feet, the nervous energy in the air; it was just what she needed.

She heard her phone ring, saw that there was no caller ID, so it wasn't her friend Marie-Agnès, busy with her restaurant in Lyon. Hardly anyone else had her number, and she wondered *who could be calling on a Sunday morning*?

"Hello, Alex, your cousin Vital here, we met last year at Christmas."

"Oh yes, hi Vital."

Alex remembered the dinner, remembered that Charlotte had been alive then, warm, strong, the best friend she'd ever had. How she missed her. As for Vital, he'd given her a pink china tea mug and strainer in the ritual exchange of gifts. Alex had forgotten about her cousin, but now she saw him again: an ugly fat bug.

"I was wondering how you're doing, after the accident and all that."

So, Charlotte's death was just part of "all that."

"I'm fine, thanks for asking;" she waited to hear the reason for his call.

"I was wondering if you're in Paris, by any chance."

"No, I'm here at Trubenne, why?"

"Oh, that's very good, Alex. I've come across some information on Trubenne that I think you should have, and I don't want to bother Richard with it."

"And what kind of information might that be?" Her dislike of Vital growing with each phrase that he uttered.

"I'd prefer not to discuss it on the phone. I wonder if we could meet the next time you're in Paris?"

"Well, I'm kind of busy right now. Can I let you know?"

"Of course, Alex. And by the way, how is Richard? He seemed tired when I last saw him."

"That would have been right after Charlotte was killed, so I guess he wasn't feeling too great. But he's much better now, back to his old self, really."

"Great news Alex. Well, I'm looking forward to your call."

When Alex finished packing, she brought her bag into the kitchen.

"I'm all set to go."

Eugene was going to drive her to the train station at Nîmes. He looked up from the map they had been studying: "We've got plenty of time," he said and, seeing her face, added "What's the matter, you look upset."

"It's that creep Vital. Remember, when we were at Malmousque I told you he had left a message for me to call him?"

Eugene had made it a point to avoid his extended family. Their prying about his work for the FBI annoyed him, and he had sensed their resentment when he and his sister had received a substantial inheritance from their aunt, Madeleine. Of course, Madeleine was an aunt in name only. She was not a blood relative, and she could have left all her money to her pet Chihuahua, had she chosen to do so. But where money was concerned, his family viewed matters through another lens.

He mistook Alex's discomfort for his own: "If cousin Vital is a creep, you don't need to have anything to do with him, do you?"

"No, it's not that, you don't understand. Vital said he's got information about Trubenne, he thinks I should see it and he didn't want to bother Richard. And then he asked how Richard was feeling, that he seemed tired the last time he saw him. He wants me to meet him in Paris."

Richard looked up, his blue eyes meeting Alex's:

"He's a rather greedy fellow, I'm afraid. And I suspect that he's living beyond his means." This was a cardinal sin, in Richard's book. "He came to see me shortly after Charlotte's death, said that I ought to move into a retirement home and turn the management of Trubenne over to him, in exchange for a part of Charlotte's shares. I sent him packing, but I guess that's what his pitch will be when you see him."

"Well, then I don't think I'm going to bother to call him back like I said I would."

Eugene spoke up: "Forgive me for intruding into a family matter, but I would suggest that you do meet him. That way we can find out exactly what he has in mind and decide how best to deal with him."

Richard turned to Eugene: "That's excellent advice. Alexia, why don't you call your cousin when you return from Toulouse and arrange to go up to Paris to see him."

CHAPTER TWENTY-EIGHT

Rue des Arts, Toulouse

BRUNO'S DREAMS ARE MORE LUCID now. The blank faces have been filled in, and he sees Father Paul's features: the pockmarked skin, the beak-like nose, and the thin lips. He also sees his own countenance: a frightened, unsmiling child.

The images of his dreams stay with him when he is awake. Walking down the street, he sees the old priest—but he was younger then—come into his room. The hairy chest, the body odor, the alcohol-infused breath, and then the penis in his mouth, soft at first and then hard. Being touched in all his private places. He remembers the showers and the sudden searing pain between his buttocks. When he told his mother he didn't want to go on retreats, she told him how lucky he was to have those opportunities.

How did the other boys deal with the shame and humiliation? Years later, one was found hanging from the rafters in his bedroom. Another moved to Australia; he guessed that was as far away as he could get. As for Bruno, when he wasn't fighting, he leaned on a glass crutch to relieve his pain.

It has all come back to him. His lips twisted into an ironic smile. He'd fallen into the river, forgotten everything, even his name, and now he had recovered the memories hidden deep in his past. A new thought: perhaps he should be grateful to Ella and the painters. Without knowing it, they had made him whole again.

Bruno caressed the thought as he fell asleep and awoke with a start at dawn. He'd been having a bad dream, but this time, he couldn't remember anything about it. It felt like his skin was too tight for his body, and he rushed out of the apartment to grab a coffee on Place Saint-Etienne.

Haunted, no, taunted, by the same question: how to find out whether the old priest he'd seen in Gaillac was Father Paul. He couldn't just knock on the front door of the *résidence* and ask for him. He ordered another coffee and stared at Saint Stephen's cathedral, recalling how unhelpful his visit there had been. And, just like that, it came to him that he needed to return to Gaillac and ask for Father Paul at Abbaye Saint-Michel. It was so obvious; why hadn't he thought of that before?

# # #

Gaillac

Later in the day, Bruno pulled into Gaillac. The sky was overcast, the air heavy with humidity; he was sure it would rain. He parked his bike and hastened to enter the abbey. There was a handful of the usual tourists admiring the statues and the stained-glass windows, gazing up at the high vaulted ceilings. Bruno made his way down the central aisle and sat in one of the pews as he looked around for someone he might ask about Father Paul. Then, he saw them: three black-robed figures kneeling in prayer in the front rows. Could one of them be Father Paul? He got up and walked to the end of the pew to get a better look at the three men. His pulse quickened as he recognized the face that he knew so well. The prominent nose, the thinning hair swept back from the forehead, the rimless glasses; Bruno's heart raced as he stepped back into an alcove, waiting for the men to leave. When they did, he could see them clearly as they walked up the central aisle. A smile crossed his lips—more of a smirk than a smile, for it signified not joy but a profound scorn. He had found Father Paul.

# # #

Bruno stepped out of the abbey's entrance and watched the three figures as they walked back to the *résidence. A furtive image appeared*—a cloud of children surrounded the priests— then evaporated into the humid air. The front door opened as the men approached—evidently, they were expected. The door closed as soon as they were inside, and Bruno felt free to look more closely at the *résidence;* it stood on a corner, and a high iron fence painted black ran along the side street. He peered over the top of the wall and saw a few chairs scattered around a table under a large parasol. But at this time of day, the yard was empty, except for an old dog, asleep under the table. There was a door in the wall with an old-fashioned lock, the kind that opened with a large key. *I can handle that.*

Bruno looked over the wall again. The fear that he had felt all these years, the fear that he tried to drown in drink, the fear that he sought to bury with every violent encounter, that fear was gone. It was time to leave. Bruno laughed as he mounted his motorcycle, the sound echoing inside his helmet. When he returned to Toulouse, too excited to stay in his apartment, he headed to the Garonne River, where he walked along the banks. It was time to make his plans.

CHAPTER TWENTY-NINE

Toulouse

JACKIE TOOK HER CHILDREN TO the Toulouse Matabiau station to join their classmates on a school holiday trip and waited at the head of the platform for Alex's train to arrive. The first thing Jackie saw was a blond head bobbing in the sea of travelers. With one glance at Alex's casual-chic attire, she instantly regretted that she hadn't even bothered to put on a clean pair of jeans. Alex picked her friend's face out of the crowd. Jackie had managed to smile, but still, there remained the tension lines around her mouth, and the dark circles under her sad eyes.

"Hi, you look great," Jackie said as they embraced.

Alex couldn't lie: "Thanks, it's great to see you," was the best she could do.

They walked back from the station to Jackie's apartment, stopping for a drink at the small Place Saint-Georges. Alex took it all in: the cafés surrounding the square packed with those enjoying a sunny spring day, the small colorful market, and the historic buildings on the periphery.

"This is enchanting. And it's great to be back in a city again!"

"Yes, it is lovely, but it's also noisy, and I find the people to be arrogant. On the other hand, there's a great market nearby—it's really huge—and we can go there tomorrow morning if you wish."

"You don't sound too happy about living here."

"No, I'm not," and Jackie told Alex about Josh leaving her and running off with a colleague from work.

"Yeah, well, I know what that's like! But I'll bet you didn't come home one night to find your husband in bed with another woman."

Jackie stared at Alex; she didn't seem upset, in fact, she was smiling.

"Doesn't that bother you?"

"Oh, it did for a while, and then I read somewhere that holding on to anger was like drinking poison and expecting the other person to die. And I just gave it up."

"I wish I could do that. But I'm still so angry."

"I know how you feel, but what good is being angry doing for you?"

"I guess…but I'm not there yet." It was time to move on: "So, what are you doing in France? I imagined that you'd be living in Paris."

Alex disliked being questioned, and yet, wasn't that what people did when they hadn't seen each other for a while? She opted for an abridged version of her story, omitting most of the events of the past year:

"I'm part owner of an old château, along with my great uncle, Richard. We're renovating it and upgrading the vineyard. I love being at Trubenne—that's the name of the village and the château—but as I said, it feels good to be in a real city from time to time. I'm sorry to hear about your husband, but you could do worse than living in Toulouse—it looks so beautiful."

"Yes, I suppose it is. Look, why don't we drop your bag off at my place, and I'll take you for a walk by the river. You're right, there are many stunning spots here, I've just been too unhappy to appreciate them."

# # #

When Jackie saw that Alex was changing her clothes before going out to dinner, she reluctantly did the same. It was one of the first times that she'd paid attention to the way she dressed, and she was surprised at how much better it made her feel. It was still light out when they walked to a restaurant on Place Sainte-Scarbes.

Early spring was one of Alex's favorite times of the year, when the days had started to grow longer, and the air was soft and luminous. She spotted an empty table on the restaurant's terrace; "Let's grab that table before someone else realizes that it's warm enough to eat outside."

Alex stared at the menu, two thoughts fighting for attention. On the one hand, should she opt for cassoulet or Toulouse baked chicken as an entrée; and on the other hand, the realization that earlier she'd been a bit abrupt with her friend. The chicken dish won out over the cassoulet. And after the waiter took their orders, she began to tell Jackie about Trubenne. Reluctantly, she mentioned Eugene as well; she couldn't find a way to describe life at Trubenne without bringing up his name.

Jackie, who had opted for cassoulet, stopped cutting her sausage long enough to interrupt her:

"So, you've found a new companion?"

"I don't think of him that way: he's a man I'm fond of, a man that I'm living with right now."

"Fond of, not in love with?"

"Maybe, I don't know. When I first met him, Eugene told me a pack of lies. Then, as we got to know each other, he started to trust me, to be more forthcoming. But I have the feeling that he's still keeping some things to himself, and since he keeps them to himself, I don't know what they are, if you see what I mean. He's a bit of a man of mystery. In a way, it's attractive, but also frustrating. But enough about me; and you, what are your plans?"

"The children finish school in another month, and I'm going to move back to Washington. I've put the apartment up for sale, but since you like Toulouse so much, you and your friend Eugene are free to come and stay until someone makes me an offer I can't refuse."

# # #

It had been a long day. Alex was enjoying a prolonged soak in an antique claw toed bathtub. She thought about what she had said to Jackie, that she was fond of Eugene. Why wasn't she able to say that she loved him; she wondered if it wasn't his secretiveness that was holding her back. The bath had cooled, the tepid water a sudden reminder of Charlotte's death. Alex hadn't told Jackie about the murders; it was still too painful to talk about that day. She stepped out of the tub, running her fingers over the scar on her shoulder; her determination to see Jacques Mornnais punished—unspoken but intense—remained.

# # #

In the middle of the night, Alex awoke with a start, as a litany of insults, followed by raucous laughter intruded on her sleep. She pulled herself out of bed to see what was going on. Jackie joined her to watch two men kicking a sack of garbage, its contents spilling out onto the street.

"Oh shit, not again," sighed Jackie, "this keeps getting worse and worse."

One of the men entered the building across the street.

"I think that's the asshole who woke me up the other night. Watch, he's going to go up there to his apartment;" she pointed to the darkened windows facing her apartment.

They waited, but there was no sign of the neighbor across the street. After a few minutes had passed, they saw another man push a garbage bin out onto the street and wheel it around the corner. Alex thought that the man looked a lot like Bruno, but then she asked herself how many other times she'd felt that she had seen him, only to be mistaken.

"Are you okay," Jackie asked, "you have a strange look on your face. I know how annoying it is to have your sleep disturbed."

"No, I'm fine." Alex hadn't told her friend about meeting Bruno Edremal in Lyon, how Eugene had gotten involved with Bruno and had helped him to recover his memory. It really didn't concern Jackie, no need to waste time talking about a man she'd never see again; "*how like Eugene I'm becoming.*"

CHAPTER THIRTY

Rue des Arts, Toulouse

FOR ONCE, BRUNO WAS UNTROUBLED by dreams. No nightmares, no menacing images fading in and out, his memories and preoccupations momentarily safely tucked away. Then the noise from the street nibbled at his slumber. He was awake now, pulling on his jeans to run downstairs and confront whoever had disturbed him. Antoine, climbing the stairs, didn't see Bruno until he was almost upon him.

"You little shit," hissed Bruno.

The big man was rather funny, thought Antoine. With his hairy chest and bulging muscles, he reminded him of a big ape, King Kong, perhaps. His laughter was interrupted by another thought: the ape had grabbed his shoulders.

"Remember what I told you the other night?"

"Sorry man, really sorry." He tried to squirm free; Antoine thought he heard the ape say, "Too late," as he fell backward down the stairway.

# # #

Bruno looked at the body splayed awkwardly on the first-floor landing.

He listened: the people who lived on the first floor must still out for the evening, but he didn't know how much time he had. What Bruno did know was that it was best to avoid the police coming by, asking questions. He'd have to get rid of the body.

Bruno ran up to his apartment, quickly finished dressing, and although it was springtime, pulled a cap down low on his forehead. He returned to the landing and dragged the skinny body down to the entry. To one side there was a small room that was used to store the building's refuse bins. Those containers had already been placed on the sidewalk to await the early morning garbage collection, but one large bin remained. It belonged to the luxury-clothing store on the ground floor and was used to dispose of their packaging.

He sat the body up against the wall, in the space left by the refuse bins and started to go through Antoine's pockets: his cellphone, a billfold with some cash, his national identity card, his driver's license and three small green plastic envelops with white powder. Bruno shoved the contents into his jacket pocket; he'd take care of them later.

The man's head moved, and he groaned. His eyelids fluttered; they weren't open, but he wasn't dead either. *Shit.* He needed to finish this up; he placed his hands around the man's neck, found the carotid arteries and squeezed. He'd done this before, and like the previous times, it worked. Antoine's head hung down, his chin touching his chest.

Bruno peered into the large bin; it was empty. *I've already wasted enough time* he thought as he lifted Antoine's inert body and folded it into the bin. He closed the cover, wheeled the container out the front door, and turned right onto Rue Croix Baragnon, where he left it in front of a furniture store.

One less asshole to bother me, his only thought as he returned to the apartment building, but his work was not over. He wanted to look around Antoine's apartment, but he hadn't found the keys in the guy's pockets. Maybe someone else had let him into the building, or maybe the door had not been closed. Then he remembered their last encounter, saw Antoine reaching for a set of keys under the doormat. He did the same and let himself in.

He packed Antoine's clothing into his suitcase, but he didn't bother with the frozen meal containers and the remnants of tiny green plastic bags. L*et them figure that out.* Papers were strewn about the kitchen table:

spreadsheets, memoranda. So, Mr. Tipette had been working on a deal. He scooped up the papers and threw them into a Picard shopping bag. Then he shut the door quietly, replaced the keys under the mat, and brought the suitcase and the bag of papers up to his apartment. It was now the middle of the night, he flopped into bed and went back to sleep, undisturbed by dreams.

CHAPTER THIRTY-ONE

Le Mirail, Toulouse

IT WAS STILL DARK WHEN Samih Ceckin's alarm rang at five a.m., as it did every morning. His back ached: it did that every morning as well. He hit the snooze alarm and shifted his weight, trying to find the least uncomfortable position for his last minutes in bed. When he could no longer postpone the start to the day, he got out of bed, crossed the room to the kitchen space and made himself a pot of Turkish coffee.

Still in his pajamas, he stepped out onto the apartment's tiny balcony to drink the thick, potent brew. He felt surrounded by a sea of concrete, the facades of the housing project's buildings like some cold alien planet. The only color was the tall chimney of the Mirail incinerator, a beacon of red in the dark gray sky.

The incinerator. Samih knew it well. Each day he hung on the back of the garbage truck as it made its rounds in Toulouse's historic center. At each stop, he'd hop down and roll the garbage bins up to the truck, push a button to activate the mechanism that would pick up the bin and dump the contents into the truck. He'd roll the empty bin back to the sidewalk, hop on the truck and perform the same task over again. The garbage crew's terminus was the Mirail incinerator, which supplied heat and hot water to the housing project's thousands of inhabitants.

The inhabitants. A few would nod hello, but most people hurried to their destination, their eyes fixed on a point in the distance, or on the ground. He knew he was lucky to have a job, but he hated living here. It seemed to him that he must have emptied a million garbage bins by now. But there would be a million more before he could retire and return to his village in Turkey.

Mirail. His day began and ended here. How bleak this place was compared to the streets that they rolled through each day. The rose-colored buildings, the cobblestones, the refuse swept up each day by men such as him: it was another world.

He went inside, poured the rest of the coffee into his cup, gulped it down and stood under a hot shower to try to relieve the pain in his back. Then he dressed and headed for the bus garage to start another day, one that would be exactly like every other day. Or not.

CHAPTER THIRTY-TWO

THE NEXT MORNING BRUNO WALKED up to Toulouse's Matabieu train station; he'd attached the Picard bag to Antoine's suitcase, which he pulled behind him. He looked up at the departure screen and saw that there was a train leaving for Bordeaux in twenty minutes. The train was already in the station; he boarded a first-class car where a few people were already seated, walked down the aisle and placed the suitcase on a luggage rack at the back of the car. He continued walking through to the next car and put the Picard bag on an overhead luggage rack. Lastly, he slipped into the toilets and left Antoine's cell phone by the sink.

# # #

Kevin had grabbed a sandwich in the Matabieu station. He saw that the Bordeaux bound train was already on the track, found his seat and started to eat his sandwich—bits of chicken in a mayonnaise-like mixture. Kevin hadn't finished it when he felt a pain in his stomach; he realized that something was off, and he headed for the WC. The sign on the door of the toilets in the second-class car said they were out of order. The closest WC was in a first-class coach, but he was in a rush now and opened the door to the first-class toilet. After he had relieved himself, he washed his hands, and at that moment he saw an iPhone 4 on the edge of the sink. Kevin wasn't a thief, but on the other hand, he wasn't one to overlook the opportunity to acquire a new iPhone free of charge, and he slipped it into the pocket of his jeans. When he got to Bordeaux, he would remove the phone's SIM card and replace it with his own. The old SIM card was of no use to him, so he threw it away.

In Bordeaux, as the cleaning crew went through the train, they found an abandoned suitcase and a shopping bag full of papers. After the lost and found office tried unsuccessfully to contact Antoine Tipette, (his name was on the luggage tag), they wondered if the papers in the shopping bag belonged to Mr. Tipette and they called Wind Power Unlimited, the company whose name was on the documents. Eventually they reached Antoine's consulting firm. No one had seen him since last Friday, and the police were called in to investigate his disappearance.

CHAPTER THIRTY-THREE

Paris

MONDAY MORNING. VITAL VESLA DE Trubenne couldn't sleep. As his calls to Antoine remained unanswered, his anxiety grew. He went to his office, made himself a foul-tasting coffee, paced the small kitchenette and continued to speed-dial Antoine. *What was that jerk up to*? *It's all done.* Those had been his very words.

He went back into his office, turned on a station specializing in financial news and watched his computer screen as Wind Power Unlimited's share price continued to fluctuate. Something was not right. Should he sell right now, he wondered. But the prospect of the profit he'd make if the merger went through overrode his premonition that the deal had gone south. Then he saw the banner on the bottom of the television: the merger talks between Wind Power Unlimited and Mondial Matrix had reached an impasse. Almost instantly, WPU's shares started to fall.

It's all done...the words echoed in his head. Fearing the worst, he played back the last message he had received from Antoine. Listened more closely this time. The last words were garbled, but the first three words were clear: *It's all gone* the consultant had said, but dream overcoming reality, Vital had heard *it's all done*.

Later that morning, more bad news arrived when his broker called him back. Vital had bought his shares on margin, and now he'd have to pay the difference between the purchase price and the sales price. He'd made a big bet and lost. Big time. His attention now focused on making his margin call, he forgot about Antoine. Later, imagining scenarios of vengeance and punishment, he felt better; he would regain control of the situation. But like his imagined profits, the scenarios would prove to be illusory.

# # #

Neuilly-sur-Seine

The white italic letters on the green canopy read *DM Animal Hotel & Spa*. Behind the double glass doors were eight hundred square meters devoted to the care and comfort of DM's clients' fur babies. The temperature-controlled rooms, each with closed circuit TV, would have turned the homeless green with envy. The wing devoted to grooming included a pool for relaxation and rehab.

From the get-go Dominic Monteil had understood the particular relationships that Parisians had with their animals: they were a projection of who the owner was or thought that she wanted to be. So many had large dogs, Labrador retrievers being a favorite. Hunting dogs by nature, they often exhibited the signs of the stress to be expected when they were cooped up all day, only taken out for a quick walk. A stay chez DM was like going away on vacation.

Several times each day, Dominic looked in on a golden retriever named Ollie Blue. They exercised the dog regularly, but he was listless. He'd lost his appetite and whimpered occasionally. Goldens were not supposed to become depressed at DM, not at the price their owners were paying.

He checked the reservation for Ollie Blue. His owner Antoine Tipette would be coming by today to pick him up. Dominic hoped that when Ollie Blue saw Antoine, he'd jump into his arms and shed the mantle of lethargy.

Ollie Blue slipped from Dominic's mind when he was called to the front desk. A tall, wiry woman, her face red with anger, was spraying bits of spittle into the air as she argued with the receptionist.

"You *must* find room for Charlène."

"I'm sorry Madame, but we were not expecting her until tomorrow, and there's no room tonight."

"That's not possible. I insist on seeing the director."

"Certainly Madame."

Dominic strode into the reception area, smiling broadly.

"Ah, Madame Vesla de Trubenne, how nice to see you." He looked at the Persian cat in the carrier, and added, "And the lovely Charlène."

Anne Vesla de Trubenne recomposed her features, her thin lips pulled against her bright white teeth, forcing an expression resembling a smile to appear.

"Oh Dominic, I know you can help me. I'm on my way to visit some friends in the country a day earlier than planned. They're allergic to cats, so you see I must leave Charlène with you a day early, and your receptionist has said this is not possible. I'm at your mercy." A flutter of eyelids, a meek smile now.

The woman behind the reception desk started to speak:

"Dominic, I was explaining to Madame Vesla de Trubenne that we have no space available tonight. Her reservation was for tomorrow afternoon."

Dominic walked around behind the receptionist's desk and pretended to study the computer screen. Uppermost in his mind was getting the dreadful woman off the premises before she created an embarrassing scene.

"No problem, dear lady. Just leave Charlène here, I'll take care of everything."

He put his arm gently around Anne Vesla de Trubenne's shoulders. It was not easy; she was a head taller than he was, but he kept his arm across her back long enough to guide her to the doorway.

"Have a lovely time in the country, dear lady."

"Thank you, Dominic, I knew I could count on you."

Dominic phoned one of his interns: "Once you've logged Charlène in—there's already a file on her; she's a regular client—put her in the spare room. You can move her tomorrow when her room is freed up."

He turned to the receptionist: "Let me know when Antoine Tipette arrives. I want to be there when he picks up his dog."

The following day, when Dominic realized that Ollie Blue was still a guest—now one overstaying his welcome—he called Antoine Tipette, but the message went to voice mail. Dominic was starting to get pissed: he needed Ollie Blue's room, and he needed to be paid.

He called Antoine's employer and after having been given the run-around, he learned that Antoine was, well…he was missing. His papers and his suitcase had been found on a train that went from Toulouse to Bordeaux, but there was no word about his cell phone. It was all quite mysterious, and they would let Dominic know when he showed up.

Antoine Tipette. Dominic recalled a thirty-something, an ordinary looking man but very well dressed. He'd quibbled about price, but Dominic had told him that they made no exceptions, no special offers. The man had called almost every other day to ask about his dog, so it was strange that he was suddenly silent. Whatever.

Luckily Dominic had asked for a part payment when Antoine made his reservation. When Antoine didn't reappear, he decided to cut his losses and posted a notice that a Golden retriever with an excellent pedigree was available for adoption. A retired couple showed up and took Ollie Blue off his hands. They treated him well, but a few weeks later they called to say that the dog had dropped dead. *Likely cause of death: a broken heart.*

CHAPTER THIRTY-FOUR

June 2011
Aigues-Mortes

PATRICK WAS THE FIRST TO arrive in the morning. Alone in the kitchen, doing his chores, he was happiest; he hadn't seen Max—maybe it was true that he was out of the picture—and Filippo always showed up later.

The phone call had come last night. A pallet with ten twenty-pound sacks of Jasmine rice from Thailand would be delivered tomorrow. When the shipment arrived, Patrick was to call this number; a driver would come by to pick it up, and he'd give Patrick an envelope with his payment. The shipment was dropped off at the delivery entrance early in the morning. Patrick called for the pickup, hoping he could hand off the pallet before Filippo arrived. But Patrick was out of luck.

"What's that?" Filippo asked him.

"Oh, just a mistake. I've already called and asked the shipper to come and pick it up."

Filippo looked at the pallet: Jasmine rice from Thailand. He had a quizzical look but silently continued walking to the kitchen.

Later in the day, a delivery van pulled up behind Citadel Sushi to collect the shipment. It took only a few minutes, Patrick hoping that Filippo was too busy to pay attention. As Patrick returned to the kitchen, Filippo grabbed his arm, pulled him close, and spoke softly into his ear:

"I know what you're up to, you little shit. The next time there's a *mistaken delivery*, we're going to open all the fucking sacks. I'm sure we'll find more than Jasmine rice."

Patrick pulled free, "Leave me the fuck alone. It's just rice, and it's none of your fucking business."

"We'll see about that."

While he scoured the pots, Patrick thought about last night's conversation. The caller said that another shipment would arrive in a week. The chef was back to slicing fish, but *we'll see about that* sounded menacing. What would Filippo do when the next shipment arrived? Patrick tried to reach his contact, but when he called the number, it just rang.

# # #

Parc naturel régional de Camargue

The volcano of phlegm erupted, echoing through the rooms of the *mas* in the Camargue. Max Martolla spit into a tissue, lit a Marlboro, and walked outside. He sat in the shade, watching the peacocks parading across the vast expanse of lawn, the cigarette smoke soothing his throat. The sound of their calling pierced the silent, still-fresh early morning air. His gaze shifted to a pond in the distance, where the pelicans clustered. It was a setting that would have quickened a real estate agent's pulse. But Max Martolla was pissed, big time.

A fit of coughing doubled him over as he lit another cigarette. When he straightened up, he returned to his study in the beautifully renovated fifteenth-century farmhouse. The records of Citadel Sushi's income and expenses surrounded an ashtray overflowing with cigarette butts. There was no way to get around it: the restaurant was losing money. Was someone stealing from the kitchen? Or dipping into the till? Emma was useless when it came to keeping an eye on things, especially when it concerned that fucker Filippo. Max's doctors had forbidden him to smoke. They prescribed rest and enough medication to stock an infirmary in a developing country. His illness had kept him confined to his home, but now he was determined to get to the bottom of things. He had threatened to close Citadel Sushi once before, but Emma had convinced him to give it a last try. With another cigarette glued to his lower lip, he got into his Range Rover and headed to Aigues-Mortes. This time, he would sort things out once and for all.

\# # #

Patrick had received a message that there would be a delivery tomorrow. When he got to work, he saw the package on a pallet outside the back entrance. He looked inside the kitchen; oh *shit,* Filippo was already there, preparing the fish. The chef nodded and continued working. *Perhaps he didn't notice*, thought Patrick, as he went outside to call to arrange for the pickup. He was looking for the number to call—it changed with each delivery—when he felt an arm around his neck and the sharp point of a sushi knife in his back.

"I know what you're up to, you little shit," hissed Filippo.

"You're crazy, I'm not up to anything. They made a mistake again and sent the rice to the wrong address."

"Yeah, right. 'Rice,' you say? Let's just see."

Filippo released his grip on Patrick's neck. Patrick tried to stop him from slicing open the wrapping, but the chef was bigger and stronger. He pushed Patrick to one side, pulled out a package of rice, and held it just beyond Patrick's reach. The knife pierced the plastic bag, and a shower of rice fell to the ground. The fear had returned: not fear of Filippo, but fear of what Momo's friends would do when they learned what had happened: "No fuckups" was what Momo had said.

"You see, it's only rice. Leave it alone, Filippo; you don't want to do this."

"Oh no, and why not, you little piece of shit?"

Filippo's arms were mid-air—one held the now empty bag; the other had the knife —when they heard a car door slam shut.

"What the fuck" growled Max Martolla. A cigarette fell out of his mouth as he was seized by a fit of coughing; he spat out a gob of something yellow and sticky and approached the two men. Oblivious to the knife in the chef's hand, Max was within an inch of his face, and Filippo stepped back as he got a whiff of the man's foul-smelling breath. Max grabbed the empty bag:

"Jasmine rice? Even I know we don't use Jasmine rice to make sushi! What the fuck are you up to, Filippo? Trying to make a little extra by selling rice on the side?"

"No, boss, it's not like that. It's the kid, Patrick…"

"Don't give me that shit. I know a double dealer when I see one. And I'm looking right at you, Filippo. I'm giving you one last chance: shut this scheme down before I do something I might regret later."

Max turned to Patrick, "What are you doing standing there? Call the shipper and tell them to come and pick up this shit, and then how about doing a little work? That's what I pay you for, remember?"

Max coughed some more, shot a gob of phlegm into the grains of white rice, and stormed into the restaurant to shout at Emma. He was on a roll.

Filippo leaned over Patrick, "Don't you forget I know what you're up to, even if that old fart doesn't get it. Too bad we can't open all those sacks of rice—I bet we'd find something interesting, wouldn't we? Just remember that we're partners, you worthless piece of shit."

Patrick stared at the disgusting mess on the ground. He found the phone number and, trembling, made his call.

"It's me, Patrick."

"Yeah, I know."

"The shipment has been delivered."

"Good, we'll pick it up this afternoon."

"But there's a problem."

"Yeah, what?"

"Filippo, he's the chef, he took one of the bags of rice and cut it open. But only rice fell out. I'm sorry—I couldn't stop him. It wasn't my fault."

"Okay, Patrick, not to worry. We'll take care of it."

The call ended, and Patrick wondered if taking care of it meant taking care of him as well. He'd fucked up, that was shitsure.

CHAPTER THIRTY-FIVE

Toulouse

THE SUN WAS BRIGHT, THE morning air still cool as Jackie picked her way through clusters of students and walked past a trio of homeless men whose dogs were stretched out on the sidewalk. She found an empty table in a café on Place Saint-Georges, and when the waiter brought her *café au lait*, she noticed that someone had left a copy of *La dépêche du midi* on the seat next to her. It promised more soothing reading than her *International Herald Tribune*. There was limited coverage of the atrocities that accompanied the Arab Spring; the focus was on traffic accidents, a *boules* championship match, the opening of *Toulouse Plages*...and the discovery of an unidentified body at the garbage incineration plant at a housing development called *Le Mirail.*

"Workers at the Le Mirail incinerator, which provides energy for heating and hot water for all the inhabitants of the giant housing complex, recently made a macabre discovery: the body of an unidentified male, probably in his thirties. First reports suggest that the body arrived at the garbage dump over a week ago. The police suspect foul play, and tests are underway to determine the man's identity and cause of death.

# # #

Alex was trying to spend a lazy morning in bed, getting up slowly, but the fly wasn't having any of that. It buzzed around the bedroom, attacking the windows that had been closed to avoid mosquitos. When she could no longer stand the noise, she got up, opened the window and waited for the fly to find its way outside. Like the buzzing fly, thoughts of the upcoming meeting at Vital's office disturbed her tranquility. Her phone rang, it was Jackie, and a window in her mind temporarily opened, letting those thoughts escape.

"How are you, Jackie?"

"Oh, fine…"

"Yes? You sound off. Is everything okay?"

"I don't know. I just read an article in a local paper, about how they found a body at a garbage dump."

"Um, okay…"

"Remember the night you were at my place, and we saw someone wheel a garbage bin around the corner? I haven't seen that awful man who lives across the street since that night, and I was just wondering if it couldn't be him. I mean, I haven't seen the lights on in his flat since then."

"Jackie, listen to me. This is your imagination working overtime. That man could be away on holiday or on business or at his girlfriend's. We don't know. And, really, we didn't see anything."

Perhaps if the caller had been Mag, Alex might have risen to the bait and speculated on the whereabouts of the 'awful man.' But now, she didn't want to think about whether he was the body in the garbage bin. Alex felt certain that she had seen Bruno that night. And she was also sure that she wanted nothing further to do with him.

"I think the best thing is to let the police figure it out. There's no need for you to get involved."

"Really?"

"Yes, absolutely. You're returning to the United States at the end of the month, and you can leave behind whatever you imagine that you saw, which was really not anything if you think about it."

CHAPTER THIRTY-SIX

Paris

IT WAS VERY EARLY MORNING, but the sun was already up when François Tran dropped Alex and Eugene off at the station in Nîmes. They wanted to return to Trubenne as rapidly as possible, and the train was much quicker than driving to Paris. As soon as they were seated Alex leaned back and closed her eyes.

"I'm no longer an early morning person; I need to sleep a little more."

"Good idea, I think I'll do the same."

But Alex couldn't sleep; she kept thinking about Jackie's phone call. Now she was less sure that the man pushing the garbage bin was Bruno. How many times had Alex thought she'd seen him, only to discover that she was mistaken? She'd been face-to-face with Bruno only a few times, and yet it was as though his image was imprinted on her brain like some malevolent etching. It would be best not to say anything to Eugene—he'd probably think she was losing it.

Eugene's thoughts kept him awake as well. He turned to Alex — he was sure she was not asleep.

"I've been thinking about Mornnais."

Alex remained silent. If it wasn't Bruno, then it was Jacques. It was annoying how uncomfortable she felt at the mention of those two names.

"And what were you thinking?"

"That I wonder where he is."

"From what you told me, maybe he's dead."

"Possible, but I don't think so. I guess I forgot to tell you that I couldn't squeeze anything out of Kenneth Petit, you know, my contact in the Interior Ministry. If Jacques had been murdered, I think he would have told me. I'd like to try to find out."

Something else he's 'forgotten' to tell me. But he's not the only one. Sauveur Paoli's cousin Charles, who'd come up to her as she was opening the front door to Charlotte's house in Marseille—what had he said? *If I can ever be of help, please do not hesitate to call on me.* And he'd given her his card. There was no point in getting Eugene's hopes up. She'd call Charles Paoli when they returned to Trubenne, and if anything came of the call, there would be plenty of time then to tell Eugene about it.

# # #

They checked into a tourist hotel near Avenue de Wagram—their room under the eaves was so cramped that they had to bend over while showering. Eugene had been asleep in that hotel when Walter Helmann had tried to steal the counterfeit Poussin paintings. Things hadn't turned out well for Walter, but Eugene felt it would only upset Alex if he told her about that night.

After an overpriced lunch in a crowded cafe, they walked to Avenue Kléber for their meeting with Vital Vesla de Trubenne. Eugene remembered his last visit to Merv Peters' office. *Vital must have had the same decorator*, he thought, as he took in the identical thick green carpet and wood paneling. Or maybe interior design was something they studied in law school. As they were about to discover, Vital had missed the class on ethics.

# # #

Vital's face was set in a tense mask. After losing his gamble on Wind Power Unlimited's merger, an infusion of cash had gone from being desirable to a necessity. He had been paired with Alex to exchange gifts at Richard's Christmas dinner. She had given him a magnum of Saint-Emilion, whereas he'd recycled a pink china tea mug and strainer that someone had offered to his wife. Alex hadn't said very much, and he judged her to be one of those pretty, empty-headed American women who walked around Paris saying everything was a*wesome*. Her companion, who she had introduced as "my friend Eugene," had a blank expression on his face: not the brightest bulb in the box, that one.

"I'm concerned about Richard. He seems to have aged a lot in the past year. I'm sure you've noticed how forgetful he is, so distracted. Not always quite there, if you get my meaning."

When Alex and Eugene remained silent, he continued:

"Frankly, we think that Richard is getting too old to manage his affairs. It might be best to start proceedings to establish a guardianship. And, as I'm a lawyer, we thought that it would make sense for me to be named the guardian."

"And just who is 'we?'" asked Alex.

"Why the family, of course."

"Vital, I can't say that I agree with you. I think Richard is perfectly fine, and he certainly doesn't need anyone to be his guardian.

"Well, Alex, I'm sorry that you feel that way."

Alex's cheeks turned pink, but she kept her voice low: "Vital, if you had me come all the way up to Paris to tell me that you're going to try to be named his guardian, then let me tell you that I will stand by Richard and oppose what you're trying to do."

Vital wondered if he had misjudged Alex; he had not expected her response. But he continued according to the scenario he had already envisioned:

"I don't imagine that you or Richard want to get tied up in long and costly litigation. Believe me, this is not in anyone's best interests."

Alex again remained silent. Eugene had never seen this side of her personality: cold and in control. She was making Vital do all the work, drawing him out by staying still.

"There could be another solution, of course," responding to a question that no one had asked. "I could help manage Trubenne in exchange for a part of Charlotte's share. If I did that, I could keep an eye on Richard and participate in the renewal of Trubenne, and you'd get the benefit of my legal expertise in the bargain."

"So, you're threatening us with litigation if we don't turn over a part of Charlotte's shares. I can't tell if you're having serious money problems or if you're just a very greedy, dishonorable man. But whatever the case, the answer is 'no.' I came to France to discover my roots, but I can see that the family tree needs some pruning, *if you get my meaning*."

They stood up, and Eugene led Alex out of Vital's office. She seemed almost paralyzed by anger. Despite the warm weather, her hand felt cold and clammy. He had seen Alex's passion on display once before. He remembered the incident when she'd learned that Jacques' driver Tarek was stalking her; she had been like a cauldron boiling over. "If he wants a fight, then we'll give him a fight. I'll spend whatever money it takes. It's a question of principle."

"I understand how you feel. But I think it won't come to anything, just leave it with me."

"What do you mean, what are you doing to do?"

"Nothing violent, don't worry. But if he persists, I'll take care of our friend Vital."

# # #

Alexandria, Virginia

Eugene just couldn't help it. The need to keep things to himself when there was no need to was too strong. He knew he ought to level with Alex and tell her what was on his mind, but instead, he told her that he needed to return to Alexandria to see his sister, who had tripped on a treadmill while at the gym. She was now nursing a badly sprained ankle, and he thought a short visit might cheer her up.

"That's a good idea," said Alex, trying to squelch the thought that Eugene might be visiting an old girlfriend.

"I'll only be gone for a few days."

# # #

Kate ran to the front door to greet Eugene. She looked well, although as they embraced, it occurred to him that his sister had put on a few pounds.

"Hey, great to see you."

"Yes, but I've gained some weight."

"You ought to try doing some exercise, there's a gym not too far from here."

"Not my cup of tea, I get all the exercise I need walking around museums."

Eugene had lost track of the number of times they had had this ritual conversation, and he didn't insist.

"How long are you here for?" she asked.

"Oh, just a few days. I need to see someone downtown."

Kate didn't bother asking who he was seeing, or why. If Eugene wanted to tell her, he would, and apparently, he didn't. Three days later Eugene kissed Kate goodbye and took a taxi out to Dulles airport, where he caught the early evening flight to Paris.

CHAPTER THIRTY-SEVEN

He was seated at a table on the terrace at Chez Michel. Suddenly, Eugene Spector was whispering in his ear: You don't need to kill Father Paul; just frighten him to death. He turned to ask Eugene how he knew about Father Paul, but he had vanished. Michel came out of the café and said: listen to Eugene, before he too disappeared. When he awoke, Bruno remembered the dream. He knew *what* he needed to do, and he set about planning *how.*

# # #

Bruno headed to a kebab joint and stood in line among a group of teens waiting to order a Greek sandwich. The kids, normally boisterous and joyful, gave him a wide berth. When it was his turn, he didn't order a sandwich—he wasn't ready to inflict that mixture of meat and fat on his stomach—but showed the man behind the counter the number for the package he'd come to pick up. It was a large, flat box, and he shoved it under his armpit and walked back to his apartment. When he arrived, he unwrapped the package and carefully laid the contents on his bed. He opened his closet and removed a white garment made of cheap polyester that he'd ordered online a few days ago. He laid the garment on top of the object on his bed; it was a bit long, but it would have to do. There was a small washing machine in the kitchen;

he dumped a package of black dye into the machine, along with the garment, and when the cycle was complete, he hung the garment up to dry before taking an iron to the wrinkles. Next, he spread the garment on his bed and placed the contents of the package—a skeleton—inside the black chasuble. He knew that for the church, black was the color of mourning, the color of death, and his lips puckered into a thin smile.

Bruno opened a compact metal candy box and removed a keyring that held several large, old-fashioned iron keys; surely one would fit the lock in the side street door of the *résidence.* He clipped the keyring onto his belt, then carefully folded the skeleton and the chasuble and placed them in the box the skeleton had come in. From the refrigerator he removed a package of ground meat wrapped in pink and white patterned paper and put the package and a banana in a plastic bag. He bided his time, sipping a bottle of Badoit, his empty eyes staring at a point on the wall. The days were longer now, and he continued to wait, sipping water, his eyes vacant, as the last rays of light dipped below the horizon.

In the darkness, he started to visualize how he would proceed. It would be best to arrive at Gaillac deep into the night when chances were good that everyone was asleep. Bruno saw himself inserting the key in the lock, which offered no resistance. If necessary, he would subdue the dog with the ground beef. Finally, he would unwrap the skeleton and place it as he had imagined. Clouds had rolled in; it was a moonless, starless night, and he took that as a good omen.

It was past midnight when Bruno, wearing a black hoodie and black jeans, strapped the packages onto his motorcycle and drove to Gaillac. He parked the bike a few blocks from the *résidence* and walked up the side street. The town was as silent as a tomb, until it wasn't. A couple—he estimated them to be in their mid-twenties—had chosen to discuss their relationship right next to the door in the wall. Whatever they had consumed—alcohol, drugs, or both—removed any inhibitions that might have caused them to lower their voices or to seek a more private venue. *Fuck* thought Bruno. Not only were they in his way, but they were also going to wake the inhabitants. None of that was part of the plan. He leaned his package against the wall and placed the plastic bag with the ground beef and banana beside it. He came face to face with the couple, his presence ending the conversation. Two pairs of startled eyes looked at him, trying to figure out who he was and where he'd come from. Bruno spoke: "Move along now. You'll wake the priests, and they'll pray for your punishment." He pointed his index finger; he didn't touch either of them, but it was enough to frighten them. The man grabbed the woman's arm, "Let's get out of here," and they ran off.

Once the couple had disappeared, Bruno detached the keyring from his belt and started to try to open the lock. On his third attempt, he could feel the lock engage, but as he turned the key, the sound of metal scraping against rust rang out. He held his breath and waited, wondering if the sound had pierced the brick walls of the *Résidence.* No lights went on in the rooms overlooking the garden; the air was silent. He pushed gently on the door; it creaked on its hinges, and he wished he'd thought to bring a can of oil. *Next time.* The dog that he'd seen before was stretched out in the same place, under the table, panting gently, its eyes open. *Stay still, that's a good boy, I have a treat for you.*

He heard a car driving up the street and slipped behind the door, edging it closed. *What if the box on the sidewalk caught their attention?* But he needn't have worried, for the car kept going. With a few quick steps, he brought the box and the plastic bag into the garden and closed the door behind him. It was time to take care of the dog; he reached into the plastic bag to remove the pink and white package. The dog started to move towards Bruno, and he quickly unwrapped the package and placed it under the table. A single bark and the hound turned its attention to the late-night snack, leaving Bruno free to carry out his plan. He looked inside the plastic bag and saw that the banana was now streaked with the red juice that had escaped from the pink and white package. *So much the better,* he grinned.

In no time, he'd dressed the skeleton in the chasuble and seated it on one of the chairs. Making sure that it was visible, he placed the bloodied banana on the pelvic bones. He glanced over at the dog; it had fallen asleep. It remained only for him remove the pink and white paper—he crumpled it into a ball that he tossed into the plastic bag—and photograph the installation. The shutters on the windows overlooking the garden were closed, blocking the light from the flash on his camera. He slipped out, locking the door behind him, and walked briskly to where he'd parked his bike. With a light heart, he returned to Toulouse and settled into a dreamless sleep. When he awoke the following morning, Bruno was ready to take his next steps.

# # #

The novice was having trouble falling asleep. He'd closed the windows to escape the mosquitos' nighttime assault, but the airless room was hot and stuffy. What if he opened the window and unlatched the shutter to let in some cool night air? Hopefully, the mosquitos had already found better pickings. The dog barked—just once—but what was that all about? He pushed open the shutter, gazed down at the garden, and then closed it rapidly when he saw the intruder, afraid that the man might have seen him. He knew he was being irrational: here he was, safe in his room, whereas it was the intruder who was exposed. And yet he stood by the window, trembling. His lips moved silently, and the novice prayed to cast away his fear; when he opened the shutters a crack, he saw a pinprick of light, and then the intruder walked out through the garden door. Relieved that the man had left, he opened the shutters more widely and saw the macabre figure on the garden chair. He dared not awaken the priest-in-residence, who, he feared, would ask him too many questions. After all, the figure would still be there tomorrow morning. He closed the shutters and the windows and laid down on his bed. He tried to fall asleep and forget about the intruder, but the man's silhouette, so briefly glimpsed, would not leave him. Then, as he called up the terrifying image in the garden below, a lone mosquito paid him a visit, and he remained sleepless until daybreak.

CHAPTER THIRTY-EIGHT

July 2011

BRUNO ROSE EARLY THE FOLLOWING day, ready to take his next steps. Out on the sidewalk, he was headed to a print shop on the outskirts of Toulouse when a garbage truck rumbling by brought a familiar smirk to his lips. But as he walked to his motorcycle, his past life threw a monkey wrench into his plans. He hesitated before answering, then decided it was better to take the call and continue on his way.

"There was a problem with the last delivery."

"Oh yeah?"

"Some guy opened one of the packages. Lucky for us, it was only rice."

"What about the pickup?"

"Already done. You'll need to meet the van, same as before, but then we need to take care of that guy."

"Who's that?"

"You know, we had a dumb kid. All he had to do was call for the pickup when the rice arrived. But the guy who works with him—a chef called Filippo—he stuck his nose into the kid's business. So, we were hoping you could tie up that loose end."

The trip to the print shop slipped to the back of Bruno's mind as he listened to the caller.

"Okay, so where do I find his guy?"

"They both work at a place called Citadel Sushi, it's outside Aigues-Mortes."

Citadel Sushi. Bruno remembered the place. He'd gone there when he was looking for the son of Sandra's colleague Caroline.

"I'm in Toulouse right now, so tell your man to wait for me. Same place?"

"Yeah. And thanks, Bruno.

# # #

Aigues-Mortes

Patrick stood at the back entrance to Citadel Sushi, waiting for the pickup. He heard Max yelling at Emma and Filippo and wondered if he would be the next to feel Max's wrath. But did that matter? Patrick imagined that he'd be shot, or that the driver would give him a beating. In fact, nothing happened. The man came, loaded the pallet into his van, and drove off. He hadn't given Patrick an envelope, but he couldn't blame them for that. He was glad to be left unharmed.

As he went inside to wash pots, Patrick thought back to Emma's phone call and wished that he were back at McDo. When she called, he would have told her sorry, I can't help you. Arguing with Véronique or begging his mother for just one more loan: anything would be better than being in the kitchen at Citadel Sushi. Why was it, he thought, wherever I am, I wish I were someplace else? He had no answer to that question.

# # #

As before, Bruno went to Côte Pavé. But this time, after he delivered the shipment, he kept the van and drove to Aigues-Mortes. By the time he arrived, it was the end of the day, and he checked into a cheap hotel on the town's outskirts. A clock in the form of a ship's wheel hung behind the reception desk, surrounded by old fishermen's nets, and signal flags decorated the lobby's walls. The maritime theme continued in his small room where he examined his face in a mirror surrounded by seashells. *If you can't live the life, you can always pretend.*

Should he go to Citadel Sushi for dinner? He thought better of it—the owner might remember when he had come looking for Patrick Trabert—and settled for a meal of rubbery mussels and soggy fries.

Early morning. It was going to be hot today, the sun's warmth already piercing the morning air. Bruno walked past the breakfast room, where prints of sailing ships hung on the walls; the walls were painted pale yellow with blue and white trim. Eighteen months ago, the cheery décor would have sent him looking for a drink, but today he left, walked into the café across the street and ordered a double espresso and a slice of baguette slathered with butter.

He could have walked to the restaurant, but instead he drove, parked across the street from the delivery entrance, and waited. At eight-thirty a.m. he saw a figure on a bicycle approaching. Could that be the dumb kid? He took a closer look as the rider passed him. Bruno didn't smile or laugh very often. But he chuckled now. It was indeed Patrick, the son of his sister Sandra's colleague Caroline Trabert; they had gotten to know each other quite well in Marseille.

An hour later, a beat-up Nissan Micra pulled up. Filippo prepared for the day by scowling as he got out of his car. Another jolt ran through Bruno's body. Filippo had been working as a chef in another restaurant when Bruno was looking for Patrick, and it was Filippo that had sent him to Citadel Sushi. No one else showed up until Emma arrived later in the morning, at the same time as the wait staff, and he was sure he'd found the nosey guy and the dumb kid that his caller had described.

# # #

Patrick was doing his best to avoid Filippo, but he knew it was just a matter of time before the chef caught up with him. He had tried not to think about yesterday's events, but seeing the look on Filippo's face, he knew that he needed to figure something out. The chef was still busy when Patrick told

Emma that he needed to go home and lie down, his head was killing him.

"I'll work extra hours tomorrow, I promise."

He was already headed to the delivery entrance when she called after him, "Okay, but I'm counting on you to make up the time tomorrow."

Outside it was a lot cooler than in the restaurant's kitchen, but he could feel the heat rising from the pavement as he pedaled slowly down the deserted road. He felt tired, worn down by work but above all by fear of the unknown consequences of yesterday's fuck-up. "It wasn't my fault," he'd said, but had they heard him, did they even care? One thing was certain: he had messed-up big time, and Momo and his friends wouldn't like that.

Lost in his thoughts, he didn't hear the van until it came level to him and forced him into the drainage ditch that ran alongside the road. It hadn't rained for weeks, and the ground was as hard as concrete. Patrick slowly struggled to his feet, the fear clogging his lungs and wrapping itself around his body like a straitjacket. He looked at the van: had it been parked outside the delivery entrance? He couldn't remember. *They're going to kill me.* He felt the tears running down his cheeks, didn't try to stop them, *what difference does it make now, anyway?* He couldn't bring himself to look at the man who was getting out of the van—he saw only a pair of dirty white sneakers. And waited to be shot.

"Hello kid, it looks like we meet again."

That voice. It was the man from Marseille, Bruno. He was the one who'd given him a beating, the man whose sister had lost her job when his mother had made off with two million euros from the bank where they worked. Now he was sure that he wouldn't be shot. He'd be beaten to death. Paralyzed by fear, he lost control of his bladder, just as he had in Marseille. He waited for the first blow to land, but instead he felt an arm hoisting him out of the drainage ditch.

Bruno pulled him against his chest before pushing him to the front of the van. Patrick glanced at his face; was it his imagination, or was Bruno smiling?

"Get in, I'm not going to hurt you, but you need to tell me exactly what happened. As you can imagine, people are upset."

Bruno loaded the bicycle into the back of the van. He asked Patrick where he was staying, and they drove to his studio. Patrick changed into clean clothes, packed up his few belongings, and they left the bike outside the door. Patrick got back into the van and stared without focusing. He had no idea what Bruno was going to do and felt powerless to stop him.

Bruno drove to Grau-du-Roi, and then to La Grande Motte. Shook his head as he stared at the truncated pyramids silhouetted against the sky:

"Fucking ugly, aren't they?" he asked.

"What?"

"Those buildings, someone should blow them up."

Patrick wasn't sure what he was supposed to say. Then Bruno seemed to have lost interest in architecture and said: "So, tell me what happened yesterday." He listened as Patrick recounted the events in the parking lot. Bruno ignored him when he whined "it wasn't my fault," and instead asked about Filippo: what did he look like, how long did he work each day?

"He puts in a long day, we all do. That's the problem. He saw me at the first pick-up, and he knew something was up. He wanted in on the action. And then the second time, like I said, he sliced open a bag of rice, right in front of Max. But I told that to your, um, friends."

"And what about you, kid? What are you going to do?"

Patrick swallowed hard. A sliver of pride had returned. He tried to stop his voice from squeaking like a machine that needed oil.

"I can't go back to the restaurant. Max will probably fire me again if Filippo doesn't stick a sushi knife in my ribs first. And they owe me money, which I'll never see."

He was close to tears again. Maybe Bruno was going to kill him after all. "Where are we going?"

"I'm taking you to Montpellier, you can get a train to Paris there."

"So, you're not going to kill me?"

"No Patrick, I'm not going to kill you," he sneered. It was the first time Bruno had spoken his name. He continued as though there was nothing unusual in the words he had just uttered: "Your girlfriend, is she continuing her father's antique business?"

"Not really, she's just selling off the inventory, bit by bit."

Bruno continued to speak; it was only a few phrases, but he was no longer asking questions.

"You've got to stop fucking around; you need to get your shit together. Your girlfriend, it gets on her nerves that you're like a leech, sucking money from her and from your mother." Patrick remembered the look on Véronique's face when Bruno and Eugene Stokes had confronted him and his mother at the house on Traverse Paul. He guessed Bruno had seen that look as well.

When they stopped at a red light, Bruno reached into his pocket, pulled out a roll of 500-euro bills, and counted out five.

"Here, this will get you started. Go back to Véronique. Tell her you'll be meeting someone who may want to help her grow her business."

The light turned green, and Bruno was silent again. When they got to the station, he checked his phone.

"Still at the same number?" By now too numb to speak, Patrick nodded.

"Okay, keep your phone charged. You'll get a call in a few days."

Patrick got out of the van, took his backpack and his suitcase, walked into the Montpellier train station and purchased a ticket to Paris. Bruno drove back to Aigues-Mortes, where he had some unfinished business to tend to.

CHAPTER THIRTY-NINE

Aigues-Mortes

FILIPPO HAD SLEPT FITFULLY. HIS afternoon nap was supposed to get him ready for the evening shift, but he kept reliving the scene outside the delivery entrance. Max looked pretty bad, smelled worse. Perhaps he'd die soon? When Filippo didn't see the kid, he asked Emma, and she said that Patrick had a severe headache; he'd taken the afternoon off. Right. The kid was probably on the phone with his low-life friends. Well, he'd take care of him tomorrow and make it clear that they were partners.

# # #

While Filippo ruminated, Bruno was on his way back to the restaurant. The sky was still bright, the air shimmering in the heat. The van was old, there was no AC, and he'd rolled down the window. As the hot breeze flew in, the memory of a hot summer night many years ago arose. It was a sleepless steamy summer night in Lyon, the sheet under his back was damp with sweat. He saw Father Paul walk into his room and approach his bed, and…he swerved to avoid a boy on a motorbike that had shot out from a side street. This time the memory didn't fade, and with it, his anger returned, and he remembered what he needed to do once he'd taken care of things for his friends.

# # #

It had been a long day. With the hot weather, people chose to dine out, and Citadel Sushi didn't stop serving until eleven p.m. The sun had set, the dark sky was punctuated with pinpricks of distant stars.

Bone tired, Filippo walked slowly across the deserted parking area and slipped into his car. He started the engine, turned the AC on to hi and leaned his head back, waiting for the blast of cold air. He never felt the chill caress, heard only the words "better to mind your own business," as Bruno's hands closed around his neck. Filippo tried to pull the fingers away, but Bruno saw only Father Paul and squeezed harder. By the time it was all over, the AC had kicked in, and Bruno, his anger spent, stretched out on the rear seat for a few minutes. Afterward, he shifted Filippo's body to the passenger seat, got behind the wheel and drove the car to an empty parking lot a few kilometers up the road. Tomorrow vendors would be coming to sell produce here, but for now, the place was deserted.

Bruno didn't bother to look at Filippo as he set fire to the car; their momentary connection had ended when he'd snapped the man's neck. He jogged back to the van and called the man in Marseille to let him know that he'd done his part, and the rest was up to them. Then he drove to Nîmes where he spent the night before returning to Toulouse.

CHAPTER FORTY

EMMA HAD NO MORE TEARS to shed. She'd arrived at the restaurant to discover the perplexed faces of the wait staff: no Filippo, no Patrick. Her stomach had contracted into a tight ball even before she called Max, and it only got worse when he started to curse.

Emma left messages for Filippo and Patrick, but something told her she'd never see either of them again. Max pulled into the parking area, the cigarette hanging from his lower lip fell on the ground as he coughed his way into the restaurant.

He went into the office, closed the door behind him and called the woman who did the books part-time. She had always had a soft spot for Max; he'd been good-looking before he'd fallen ill. She arrived a few hours later and together they went through the accounts. As he'd suspected, it looked like some of his suppliers had overcharged him, and he wondered if all the cash receipts had been logged into the register. But there were no invoices for Jasmine rice, no record of any transaction. He lit a cigarette, was shaken by a fit of coughing, stomped it out on the floor.

"Are you all right?"

"Yeah, just a bit under the weather. Thanks for coming over."

"Anything else I can do?"

He sighed and shook his head. So, Filippo had been cheating him, but he'd also been right about the kid. It seemed hard to believe that the kid was mixed up in something shady, but he guessed that he was. His first thought was to call the police, but did he really want them sticking their noses into his business? And what difference did it make now? He heard a noise outside his office. It was Emma who'd been knocking, she was now standing in the open doorway: "Are you OK?" she asked.

Max's forehead was damp; the perspiration gave his face a grayish sheen. He slumped back in his chair, exhausted. It would take too much of his energy to even light another cigarette.

"I'm fucking *not* OK. And I'm too sick to go on with this any longer. We're closing the restaurant for good. It's over. Tell everyone to leave, we'll send them a letter or whatever and the money we owe them."

# # #

Max was sitting on the patio of his *mas*, a *pastis* in one hand and a cigarette in the other when the Gendarmes showed up. A man and a woman: she took the lead. They had found the carcass of a partially burnt car: it was registered to his chef, Filippo Panatino. There was a body in the car that they would need to identify.

"Well, he didn't show up at work today."

"Do you know anyone who would wish him ill," asked the woman.

When he finished coughing, Max sipped some of his *pastis:* "I wouldn't have a clue. I'm hardly ever at the restaurant these days, I'm dying, you know."

The Gendarmes looked at their feet, then the woman handed it over to her colleague. "We understand that someone named Patrick Trabert is missing as well."

"Oh yeah, wimpy kid, he washed dishes and cooked rice. Not the sharpest tack."

"We'd like to talk to him, any idea where he might be?"

"Sorry, I can't help you there. Did you ask my wife, she's probably got his phone number."

Max inhaled deeply, and as the phlegm rattled around his throat, the Gendarmes bid him a pleasant evening.

\# # #

Fontainebleau

The next day, Patrick had a visit as well.

“I couldn’t stand the work anymore,” he told them. “So, I went home, packed my stuff and hitched a ride to Montpellier where I took the train back up to Paris. I think I still have my ticket if you want to see it.”

The CCTV in Montpellier showed Patrick at the ticket window: he was alone. And the conductor had checked his ticket on the train, which had pulled into Paris at about the time Filippo had left work.

After the police left, Patrick turned to Véronique and smirked: “I’ve got a pretty good idea about what happened to Filippo. He deserved what he got. I wish I could have been there. Not that I’d ever tell the police.”

He looks the same she thought, *but he’s different. Something happened. It’s like he’s finally grown balls.* She took his hands in hers and stood close to him, pressing her breasts into his chest.

“Why don’t you come upstairs and tell me all about it?”

CHAPTER FORTY-ONE

FATHER PAUL WOKE UP BEFORE dawn; the demands of his aging body sent him to the toilet, and when he returned to his bed, he couldn't fall back asleep in his airless room. He should have been at ease, hidden away in the *résidence,* yet he felt a vague discomfort. The heat here in Gaillac was oppressive, yet it was no different from the summers he had spent in Lyon, and he'd not been particularly bothered by the heat at the *Centre d'Etudes.* He opened the shutters to let in a whiff of cool night air, barely glancing at the garden below, still shrouded in darkness. Stretched out again on his bed, he waited for a refreshing breeze to comfort him, but all that he felt was a nameless, diffuse anxiety.

# # #

The skeleton was discovered in the early morning hours when the novice came to take the dog for its first walk of the day. Father Joseph, the priest-in-residence, might have been impressed by the novice's calm demeanor; he couldn't have known that the boy had had all night to come to grips with what he had seen.

Father Paul had joined the other residents who had gathered in the garden. The group stood rooted in place, paralyzed, struck dumb by the apparition. All eyes—except those of Father Paul—were riveted on the skeleton. A low murmur arose: 'blasphemous,' 'sinful,' 'obscene.' The effigy was removed from the garden and placed in a garbage bin. Later that morning, a prayer was offered to purify the garden. The inhabitants of the *Résidence*, like a flock of aged penguins, had assembled in the meeting room; it was a monochrome scene—all black, brown and white. "What is the meaning of this sacrilege," Father Joseph asked the assembled group. Was it a random stunt of nastiness, or was there some deeper meaning behind how the skeleton was displayed? His gaze swept over the attendees; some had their eyes cast downward, others' faces were devoid of emotion, and a few mumbled expressions of horror and the need to punish the wrongdoer.

Father Paul shivered in his black robe despite the July heat. Through the fog of words circulating around him, the image of the man on the motorcycle arose, and the muscles in his belly tightened. At the time, he'd thought the man looked like Bruno Edremal, and now he again wondered if it had been him. Another nagging thought arose: only one person could have placed the horrible effigy in the garden—Bruno Edremal. As their leader had suggested, putting the skeleton in the garden was no random act of nastiness. Father Paul understood only too well the deeper meaning that the priest had alluded to, and he wondered what Bruno would do next, for he was sure there would be a next time. It was so unfair: what had been the point of traveling to Gaillac if his hiding place was so easily discovered? He could hardly ask the church to move him again, and yet, at the thought of remaining in Gaillac, he felt the cold stab of dread in his innards.

As Father Paul tried to stifle his increasingly fearful thoughts, Father Joseph announced that the diocese had arranged for the residents to spend the remaining weeks of summer in an old chalet in the Pyrénees. Perhaps by the time they returned, Bruno would have forgotten about him; he hoped God would hear his prayers.

CHAPTER FORTY-TWO

THE LOOSE END TIED UP, Bruno returned to his plans to punish Father Paul and headed southeast to Narbonne. When he arrived two hours later, he didn't linger in the historic city center but followed the road to an industrial park on the outskirts. When he drove up to a low-lying concrete building and saw the sign *Imprim'Narbonne* that hung over the plate glass windows, he knew he'd found what he was looking for: a random print shop with so many clients that his job would go unnoticed.

"How can I help you," asked the woman at the reception desk. Bruno noticed that she was wearing a blonde wig, with a fringe of black hair visible at the base of her neck; he tried not to stare and shifted his gaze to her mouth, a deep pink slash in her face. "I have a photo, and I'd like to print some posters from it," he said to the mouth. She slid an order form across the desk, "Fill this out, please."

An hour later, he took the cardboard tube containing the posters he had ordered, got on his bike, and returned to Toulouse. He was pleased that all was going according to plan, but that was before he arrived in Gaillac the following day.

# # #

It was late afternoon when Bruno crossed the Tarn, a deep blue gash between the riverbanks, and rode into Gaillac. Where was the municipal billboard, where posters advertised local concerts, garage sales, and meetings of clubs and associations? He rode around until he'd located the billboard, and although it was not part of his plan, he felt drawn to the *Résidence Saint-Michel.* He parked his bike behind the Abbey and walked behind a small group of tourists who exited the building under a cloud of fragrant summer air. As the group passed in front of the *Résidence,* Bruno realized something was different: all the shutters on the ground floor were shut. Had they closed the shutters to escape the afternoon heat? He left the group and walked around the building, trying to find a sign of life, but all was still aside from the hum of the cicadas. If only he'd brought his keyring, but he hadn't.

"*Merde*," he grumbled.

He came to the front of the building and noticed the sign taped to the front door: *Fermé jusqu'au 1er septembre.*

Where could they have gone? Bruno felt confused. The black curtain had returned, rising and falling on the façade. All he could think of was to walk into the Abbey; he shuffled aimlessly around, looking for an answer, but none came. Back outside, he saw a workman tending to a flowerbed.

"I'm looking for my nephew, I was told he was at the *Résidence Saint-Michel*, but it looks all closed up. Do you know where they've gone to?"

The man stopped trimming away dead leaves, mopped his brow, and looked up at Bruno: "Ah, that lot, they've gone away for the summer, too hot for them here. Your nephew, he'll be back in September."

He lowered his head and continued working. The conversation ended, and Bruno realized that his plan would have to wait until September.

# # #

Toulouse was like an oven. He thought he'd head down to the coast and spend some time at the beach, waiting for the summer to end. But first, it was time to go to Lyon to check on Sandra's mail.

The summer heat had settled on Lyon as well, but he realized how much more at home he felt here than in Toulouse. That was only normal;

he'd grown up in Lyon, whereas Toulouse was just a chink in his memory. At Chez Michel, the brightly colored tables were set out under the trees. When Bruno saw the waiter, he remembered his own time working at the café. Life had been simpler when he'd lost his memory, but he felt more complete now that the blanks had started to be replaced by names and places.

Bruno felt comforted by the sameness of it all: the trees on the little square, the furniture, and Michel himself, unloading the dishwasher. He came out from behind the bar to hug Bruno, and ask how he was doing, although Michel knew that he wouldn't get much out of him. He handed Bruno a few pieces of junk mail; "You can put those in the garbage, but as long as I'm here, how about your *Salade Lyonnais*?"

He sat at a purple table on the café terrace and ordered a bottle of Perrier. While he waited for his meal, he leafed through a copy of *Le Progrès* that someone had left on an adjacent table. When he got to the Dining section, a rare smile softened the hard lines of his face: Marie-Agnès and Tomas, owner-chefs of a restaurant called Chez Blondie, were smiling back at him. So that was what the red-haired cow was up to! He wondered if Jacques Mornnais knew. Of course, Jacques had lost interest in Marie-Agnès a long time ago, so it probably didn't matter—especially since Jacques hadn't been heard from since he disappeared last February.

He skimmed the article, learned that the restaurant's offerings could be delicate, crisp, moist, slathered, and infused; a sauce embraced vegetables; the butter swirled, and textural delights abounded. Had it not been for his past acquaintance with Marie-Agnès, he would have passed. But his curiosity was piqued. He decided to make a reservation; he hoped that there would be no hard feelings.

CHAPTER FORTY-THREE

August 2011
Lyon

MARIE-AGNÈS WAITED HER TURN to buy tomatoes. The old couple that ran the stand had the best offering in the Croix-Rousse market. There were big, meaty beefsteaks, varieties of pale red and yellow and brown, deep red round tomatoes, green tomatoes, yellow, red and orange cherry tomatoes. She would choose only the best for Chez Blondie. The woman took the time to talk with each client, and the Parisian in Marie-Agnès wished that she'd hurry up. She practiced patience, examined the dress and sandals of the woman in line in front of her, noticed the tanned arms and the blond ponytail…and felt a twinge of guilt as she thought about Alex for the first time in months. *How could I have forgotten about her? What kind of a friend am I?*

Marie-Agnès had gone to the hospital in Marseille to be with Alex in the aftermath of the horrible shooting on Sauveur Paoli's boat. After Charlotte's funeral, Alex and Eugene had returned to Marseille, but they were now spending the summer at Trubenne, or so she thought. At first, they had called each other regularly, but as the time when by, the calls became less frequent.

It was her turn. She bought some tomatoes for salads and another variety for sauces and hurried back to the restaurant and called Alex. The words came tumbling out: "I can't believe that it's already been a year since you first visited me in Lyon. I miss you, even if I haven't called; it's just that we've been so busy with the restaurant. You and Eugene must come for a visit."

Marie-Agnès. She'd been mugged in the metro, thanks to Bruno and Jacques, but instead of destroying her, it had made her stronger. "I miss you too. Let me check with Eugene, and I'll call you right back."

# # #

Eugene was enthusiastic about accepting Marie-Agnès' invitation. Alex didn't talk about Charlotte's death, but he knew she'd been deeply affected by it. He'd tried to encourage her to meet people, make friends. She'd gone to Toulouse to re-connect with an old acquaintance from Washington DC, but the woman was depressed and anxious, and he wasn't sure that much good had come from that visit.

"We can stay with Marie-Agnès and Tomas," she told him.

"I guess we could, but wouldn't you rather stay in a hotel, and have a bit more privacy?" He put his arms around her and drew her close "What do you say, Alex, shall we splurge?"

Her eyes shone, "Yes, let's do that."

"Oh yeah, and you'll have to meet my friends Travis and Julie, they live in Lyon, and they've got a chalet at La Clusaz. We'll have to go skiing with them this winter."

Alex felt a warm wave of joy: Eugene was finally sharing with her.

# # #

Icy black slope ski instructor with pink hair the ski lift that got stuck *fondue savoyarde* La Clusaz their chalet the snowfall the lines French school holidays too many children too many people…

Alex sat quietly as the cloud of words swirled around her, waiting for Eugene, Travis, and Julie to stop talking about the time they spent skiing together. She smiled, sipped her wine and wondered how long it would take before they exhausted the topic. She'd never been good at small talk, but couldn't they at least try to include her in their conversation?

Travis had insisted that Alex and Eugene stop by for dinner. He was glad to see Eugene, but mostly he was curious to meet his mysterious companion. Yet they'd gone on and on about La Clusaz, and suddenly, Travis noticed that she'd said nothing.

"Sorry for going on like that, Alex. Would you like some more wine?"

She looked at her glass: it was empty. If she weren't careful, she'd be drunk before the end of the evening.

"No thanks, I'm okay."

Eugene cut in: "In a few years, Alex will be producing her own wine."

"Oh really?"

"Yes, we're renovating an old family château and upgrading the vineyards. But there's still a lot of work to be done."

Alex's eyes sparkled as she talked about Trubenne, about her uncle and their project. When she had sat silently, Travis judged her to be just another attractive blonde, but when he heard the excitement in her voice, he could sense why Eugene had been drawn to her.

Julie got up to go into the kitchen. Alex followed her: "Please, let me help."

Eugene looked at Travis:

"I take it you approve?" he laughed.

Travis grinned: "It sounds like you've got your work cut out for you; I can only imagine how much there is to do in a place like Trubenne."

"Yeah, but it's got a lot of potential. In fact, one of Alex's cousins, an obnoxious lawyer — you know the type — tried to pressure her into turning over a share in the property. Of course, she brushed him off, but I don't think he's going to take 'no' for an answer. I have a feeling that he's got secrets, things that he'd like to keep hidden, and I was wondering if he's ever crossed your radar."

"What's his name?"

"Vital Vesla de Trubenne."

"I'll take a look and let you know. But you'll have to pay dearly, my friend: I won't settle for anything less than a bottle of the fine wine that Alex is getting ready to produce."

"Lucky for me that you're a patient man. Thanks."

They started dinner with gazpacho, followed by cold poached salmon and tender green asparagus and ended with a chilled raspberry mousse.

Alex was radiant. After the evening's false start, she felt at ease with Travis and his wife. Eugene too was pleased. Alex was happy—she was so beautiful when her face was relaxed. As for Vital, he'd told Alex not to worry, and he wasn't going to let her down.

CHAPTER FORTY-FOUR

Lyon

CHEZ BLONDIE WAS A SMALL RESTAURANT, and everyone pitched in to do a bit of everything. One of the waitresses answered the phone and took a reservation for a Mr. Bruno Leblanc for eight p.m. tonight.

When Alex awoke that morning, she suddenly realized that although she'd been in France for over a year and a half, she'd not visited a single museum. She felt a surge of energy after last night's dinner and decided to start making up for lost time today. They started out at the Textile Museum, and after lunch returned to La Croix-Rousse to visit the Silk Museum, *La Maison des Canuts.* Eugene would have preferred to jog along the quays but instead allowed himself to get swept along in Alex's exploration of the history of Lyon's silk industry. They returned to their hotel in the late afternoon.

"That was fun, wasn't it?" she asked.

"Well, in case I hear anyone refer to the '*canuts,*' at least I'll know what they're talking about."

She giggled as he put his arms around her and nuzzled the warm space between her shoulder and her neck. An hour later they showered. Eugene gently soaped Alex's body from head to toes; then it was her turn.

"I'm cold, aren't you," she asked as they moved from the steamy bathroom into the bedroom's chill air.

"Very," he laughed and pulled her under the covers where they stayed until it was time to go to dinner.

# # #

When Marie-Agnès was preparing to open Chez Blondie, she had asked Li, the art forger that had been employed by Jacques Mornnais, to decorate one of the restaurant's walls. One could only appreciate Li's sense of humor: he'd done a mural in the style of Le Nain Frères, using the likenesses of the inhabitants of the Château d'Hélène: Jacques Mornnais, his wife Mila, Tarek the driver, and Bruno Edremal. Even Marie-Agnès, who'd spent only one night at the château, was there.

When Bruno arrived, he was seated along the wall facing the mural.

"Would you like an aperitif, Sir?"

"Just a Perrier with a lemon slice please."

He felt the bubbles soothe his throat and tickle his nose as he stared at the mural and smiled. The painting must have been done by Li or Wen. He was certain about that. How else would those faces have found themselves in a seventeenth-century setting? So, the red-haired cow had been in touch with the painters: that might be helpful.

# # #

Eugene and Alex arrived at Chez Blondie a few minutes after Bruno. Eugene felt Alex's hand tighten around his wrist as they entered the restaurant—she had seen the mural before he did.

"What is it, are you OK?"

"Look at the wall" she whispered. "I'd forgotten about that mural. It's the one that Li did for Marie-Agnès. I still can't believe that he peopled it with Jacques and his entourage. He even included Mag!"

"Indeed! I think it's quite amusing, and she probably does too." Some of the faces were familiar to Eugene: Jacques, Bruno, Mag, and even Mila. He remembered the time he had briefly crossed paths with her, but he didn't mention that to Alex.

Bruno had continued to stare at the painting as Alex and Eugene were shown to a table along the wall with the mural. There they were again, the blonde and Eugene, the American. He nodded and pursed his lips in a smirk, the unpleasant smile a sign that he was enjoying himself.

Eugene formed his mouth into a smile as well. Not a smirk, but a bland upturning of the corners of his lips. For a moment, Alex held her breath as she looked at Bruno's smug countenance. Yes, she had indeed seen him that night in Toulouse. She exhaled, and like Eugene, managed to pretend to smile.

"What do you suppose he's doing here? Can we never get away from him?"

"Well, remember that his sister lives here, and he's from Lyon originally, so it's not that surprising, although I would not have expected him to show up in Marie-Agnès' restaurant, of all places."

"Weird guy."

"Yeah, but let's not let that spoil our dinner."

And dinner was an engrossing affair. After a starter of *pâté en croute,* Eugene decided to sample another Lyonnaise specialty: *le tablier de sapeur,* or boiled tripe in wine sauce. It tasted much better than it sounded. Alex, less adventuresome, opted for a Bresse chicken with truffles.

Tomas walked through the restaurant, chatting with the diners. He stopped at Bruno's table, even though he remembered Mag telling him that Bruno had tried to have her killed.

"I was admiring your mural. Who is the artist? Someone from around here?"

Tomas looked more closely at Bruno. It appeared that his was one of the faces on the wall. He gave Bruno the same answer he had given to Jacques when he'd asked the same question:

"I wish I could help you. It was a Polish fellow, one of those posted workers, just passing through. Never did get his name straight. So sorry."

Bruno smirked again. "Not to worry. It's not important."

The doors to the kitchen swung open, and Marie-Agnès made a beeline for Alex and Eugene's table. "I'm so happy to welcome you," as she leaned over to embrace Alex.

"Don't look now, but that dreadful man Bruno is sitting across from us," said Alex.

Alex felt Marie-Agnès' fingers dig into her shoulder, heard the intake of breath, and then her friend straightened her back, smiled, and slowly made her way around the room until she reached Bruno's table.

"Why hello Bruno, welcome to my little *bouchon*. Was everything okay? Did you enjoy your meal?"

"Excellent. And your interior decoration is as refined as your cuisine. It's an honor to be immortalized on the wall of your restaurant. Please, tell me the name of the artist."

Marie-Agnès legs had turned into two iron girders, riveted to the floor. "I…I do not remember."

The smirk returned to Bruno's face. He spoke in a low voice, "Marie-Agnès, it's me, Bruno Edremal, please don't insult my intelligence. Was it Li or was it Wen?"

Marie-Agnès, still unable to move, looked for a way out. "Really Bruno, I cannot tell you. They came down together, each worked on a part of the mural, and I did not pay attention as to who did what."

"At least you're not giving me that bullshit about a Polish posted worker."

"No, Bruno. I would not do that. And if you will excuse me now, I have my other guests to attend to."

Marie-Agnès forced herself to move slowly, putting on a pleasant face as she continued her rounds. Li had told her that Wen had returned to China, but she hoped it would slow Bruno down if he were looking for both men rather than only Li.

After Bruno paid his bill, he came over to Alex and Eugene.

"Small world, isn't it?"

Eugene stood up and put his arm around Bruno's shoulder. "Bruno, my man, how are you?"

Eugene leaned closer, "Any idea where our friend Jacques is?"

"Afraid not, but if I hear anything, I'll be sure to let you know. We're still a team, aren't we?"

"You bet."

"Okay then, I'll call you. You're still at the same number?"

Eugene nodded, they shook hands, and Bruno walked out. He turned around once and waved, and then he was gone.

The restaurant had started to empty out. Tomas and Marie-Agnès joined them, and as they sipped tiny glasses of iced *limoncello* the conversation turned to Bruno's sudden appearance.

"I just tried to call Li, but his number's been disconnected. I do hope he'll be safe," said Marie-Agnès. She looked at Eugene, seeking reassurance.

"Let's assume he's in Paris—one of ten million people. Or he could be anywhere. So, I wouldn't be too concerned. Perhaps he ought to have thought twice before throwing Bruno into the river. You can understand that the man might be upset about that."

"But he tried to rape Ella…."

"That's not what he says. According to Bruno, he was drunk and passed out right after he caught Ella going through his jacket pockets. Anyway, there are only two people who know what happened that night—and one of them is back in the Philippines."

Alex had been savoring her *digestif,* and the cool elixir had loosened her tongue. Before she realized it, she said "I saw Bruno when I was staying with a friend in Toulouse, he came out of the building across the street from her apartment and…"

"C'mon Alex," interrupted Eugene. "You always see Bruno until it turns out that it wasn't him after all."

"But I *did* see him. He was pushing a garbage bin up the street and…" She stopped as she realized how crazy it would sound if she completed the sentence.

Eugene placed his hand gently on hers. "Okay, maybe you did see him. He's always turning up where we least expect to see him."

Alex turned to Marie-Agnès, "It was a wonderful meal, and I can see why your restaurant gets rave reviews."

"But maybe we should rethink some of the décor," Tomas gave a mirthless laugh.

"I never told you, but both Jacques Mornnais and Merv Peters came to the restaurant. And each asked about the mural. At the time Li painted it, I thought it was kind of funny, sort of a private joke. But now it doesn't seem funny at all. In fact, I'm beginning to be frightened each time I look at that wall," said Marie-Agnès, "and did you know that Merv Peters died in an automobile accident after dining here? It gives me the creeps."

Before she could stop herself, Alex added, "And Jacques Mornnais has disappeared."

"That just leaves Bruno, then. How I wish he'd disappear as well!" said Marie-Agnès.

Tomas put his arm around her shoulders, "Let's not get sucked into the orbit of those unpleasant people. We can choose not to think about them."

"I second that," said Eugene. He rose, "It's getting late, and we'd best let your friends close up. Great meal! We'll be back."

# # #

Arms around each other, Alex and Eugene walked back to their hotel. A refreshing breeze wafted up from the river:

"That bit of chill air feels good," said Eugene. The heat was starting to get to me. I'm looking forward to getting back to Trubenne."

"Yes, but it's been great to spend some time in a city. Sometimes listening to the sound of the grass growing gets on my nerves. I think you would love Toulouse. It has the most breathtaking architecture. Jackie must be back in Washington by now, but she offered me her apartment whenever we like. Maybe we could go in September when the weather starts to cool off?"

On the one hand, Eugene was dubious as to whether Alex had seen Bruno. On the other hand, his intuition told him that Bruno had some idea of Jacques Mornnais' whereabouts, but the only way to be sure was to try to squeeze it out of the man. And what if he, in fact, did live across the street from Jackie? There was nothing to lose by going to Toulouse: it would make Alex happy, she could admire the buildings, and who knows, he might find out what Bruno was doing in that city.

The effects of the *limoncello* started to wear off in the cooler night air. Alex had come to a decision. No more secrets: she would tell Eugene about the newspaper article that Jackie had read to her.

"I know it sounds far-fetched," she concluded, "but it's not impossible."

"True enough. Look, why don't we plan a trip to Toulouse in September. We can pound the pavement, breathe polluted air and see if our friend Bruno lives nearby."

"Why must we bring Bruno into the picture? Today was such a great day until we saw him."

He squeezed her closer to him. "It's still a great day, not over yet." He continued: "Remember what I told you about my being adopted. And that I think Jacques Mornnais knows something about my biological parents? And it wouldn't surprise me if Bruno has some idea about where Jacques is these days."

"All right, it's settled then. I'll get in touch with Jackie." The good news was that Eugene had confided in her. The not-so-good news was that Jacques Mornnais was still lurking at the edges of her life, a dark cloud that would not go away.

CHAPTER FORTY-FIVE

Fontainebleau

THE BAKERY WAS CLOSED. SO were the butcher, the cheese shop and the greengrocer. Along the street, "closed for vacation" signs hung in the windows of the hardware store, the newsstand, and the insurance agent. Even the Asia Garden restaurant had closed its doors. Véronique wheeled the garbage bin back from the street—at least the garbage collection continued in August.

The weather. Depressing when it was cold and gray, depressing, too, when the empty sidewalks shimmered in the silent heat of the midday sun. She was anxious to get away, to spend the month at her house in Marseille. Of course, Patrick would be with her, and she had mixed feelings about that. She'd been glad to see him when he'd turned up in July, yet irritated that, once again, he'd been unable to hold down a job. *How hard could that be*, Véronique wondered, ignoring the fact that she too had no job. But she did have the inventory that her father had left, and she'd been gradually selling off the furniture and *objets d'art*. So far, she didn't need to contemplate working at some tedious office job, but what would happen when she ran out of things to sell? Well, she'd deal with that situation when the time came.

Patrick. Since he'd returned with a pocket full of 500 Euro bills, she had agreed that he could stay for the month. When she asked, he said he'd won the money playing *Loto*. She didn't believe him, but she was used to his lack of candor.

\#   #   #

A few days ago, they had been in the kitchen, preparing dinner. Citadel Sushi had offered a traditional menu in addition to raw fish, and Patrick had watched as Filippo handled the orders. Away from the toxic environment of the restaurant's kitchen, he found that he enjoyed cooking and Véronique was happy to let him take the lead.

Six radishes floated in a bowl of cold water. He took one, dried it, and started to sculpt three petals. As he carved the first petal, his phone rang. *Oh shit.* This could only be bad news. He let the phone ring and completed the first radish flower. It looked pretty good, the petals standing away from the center, bright red and white. The phone started to ring again. *Who the fuck could that be? It was probably a telemarketer. If I let it ring, they'll give up and try another number*. The phone beeped; he had a text message: "*Answer the fucking phone, Momo*."

Patrick started to carve a second radish when the phone began to ring again. *Okay, it was not a telemarketer that was calling—it was probably Momo. If I don't answer, he'll just keep trying until he comes to kill me. What the fuck, I may as well get it over with.*

"Is that you, Patrick? Why the fuck don't you answer your phone?"

"Hi Momo, yes, it's me. I was making dinner."

"Oh yeah, what're you cooking?"

"I was carving radish roses if you must know."

Momo laughed. That was a good sign. "Fucking radish roses. Who would've thought? Well, sorry to take you away from your radishes" he sniggered, "But Bruno told me all about you and your girlfriend."

"*Fucking Bruno,*" he thought. "*So, Momo knows where to find me. Shit.*"

"Oh really, what did he tell you?"

"Enough to make me think we can do business together again. As long as your girlfriend doesn't go batshit crazy like that fuck, Filippo."

"Can we talk about this in a couple of weeks Momo? We're getting ready to go on a little holiday." But Patrick couldn't stop himself from asking, "What kind of business, Momo?"

Momo ignored his question: "You gonna go to her place, in, let's see, it's Marseille, right? Take a little vacation after all your hard work?" Momo chuckled; he was enjoying himself.

"Yes, why are you asking?"

"Just want you to relax. Too bad about that guy Filippo, but you don't need to worry about him anymore."

They've killed Filippo, and now they're going to come after me. "Uh, okay Momo, but what kind of business?"

"Oh yeah. A friend will call you in September, come to see you in Fontainebleau, explain it all to you then. I'm sure you'll do a great job this time. Great talking with you Patrick."

Véronique had been unloading the dishwasher. When Patrick's phone rang for the third time, she stopped what she had been doing and didn't try to hide the fact that she was eavesdropping on his conversation. When the call ended, she asked, "What kind of business, Patrick? And who is Momo?"

"He's just some guy that I met in Aigues-Mortes. And I don't know what kind of business. He said a friend would be calling me in September. It's probably nothing."

Véronique's mouth was open—she wasn't going to allow Patrick to brush her off so quickly—and then she brought her lips together. What was the point of grilling him when he'd only tell her more lies? She would wait until September, and if the 'business' didn't materialize, then this time Patrick would be gone for good.

CHAPTER FORTY-SIX

Vitry-sur-Seine

A CANOPY OF DENSE WHITE clouds in the stifling August heat, the air so thick you could almost wrap your fist around it to squeeze out the humidity. Li stood at the open window, feeling the rivulets of sweat run down his body. It was too hot to paint, it was too hot to do anything other than breathe and wait for the heat to pass.

The room was larger than the stall in the stable that he'd occupied at Château d'Hélène. But at least there he'd had his atelier, whereas here he lived and worked in one room. He had been more comfortable in Wen's uncle's apartment, but when his friend returned to China, Li's intuition told him that it would be better if he had a place of his own. They had never talked about the events at the château. Wen's uncle hadn't asked any questions, but Li felt that he needed to protect the man, should the police—or anyone else—come looking for him.

Everything about the house was faded: the brick façade, the shutters, the patch of lawn in the front yard, and the ragged carpet that covered the entry and the stairs. The house's inhabitants were all Asians: illegal immigrants. As they kept to themselves, for the moment the police didn't bother with them; they had other more pressing problems to deal with. In Li's room there was a bed—he'd put a board under the soft mattress—two chairs, a table, an old, noisy refrigerator, and a sink. There were a shower and a toilet in the hallway, and the inhabitants took turns with the cleaning.

The sky darkened, there was a flash of purple lightning, and a roll of thunder; all was again silent, until it started to rain. Bullet-like drops hit the windowpanes, crashed into the dry grass. Mud puddles appeared, and the temperature dropped a few degrees. Li left the window open, as well as moving the door ajar to create a draft to cool the overheated space.

Oh shit! The floor was getting wet, the water creeping towards the twenty paintings that leaned against the far wall of the room. He slammed the window shut, quickly mopped the floor, and looked around to be sure that the rain had not done any damage, for he was expecting an important visitor later today.

Friends had introduced Li to Raymond Chartrier, a computer engineer looking to enhance his life experience by promoting artists whose work spoke to him. Raymond had seen two of Li's paintings at the Chinese Cultural Center in Paris. The artist's mixture of styles—hyperrealist and Chinese—fascinated Raymond, and he made an appointment to visit Li to view his work. But there was one painting that Raymond had no need to see, and Li moved it from the far wall and put it at the back of the clothes closet.

It had stopped raining, the sun came out, and the air began to heat up. By tomorrow it would again be unbearable.

At five p.m., Li looked out the window and saw a stocky man pick his way through the puddles on the front walk. By the time he reached Li's room, Raymond Chartrier was winded, beads of sweat running down the sides of his face. He sat down to catch his breath, and Li offered him some cold tea.

"Thanks, my God I hope this weather doesn't last much longer. If it does, it's gonna kill me." He smiled, it was a self-deprecating smile, so different from the people at the château, and Li smiled back.

Li turned the paintings around for Raymond to examine.

"Do you mind if I take some photos? I want to show them to an association I work with. They're called EMC—that's short for Extra-Muros Culture—and they run cultural centers all over France. I think you'd be a perfect fit."

"You do?"

"Oh yes. Now, what's your phone number, I forgot to ask when we met."

"Uh, I lost my phone. I intend to buy another one come September."

"Let me buy you a phone. You can pay me back when you sell your first painting. But tell me something: your friends introduced you as Li, but I see the name on the door is Ma Zhen." So, if you don't mind my asking, what *is* your name?"

Li smiled. "First, thank you for the offer of the phone. Of course, I'll pay you back straight away. Ma Zhen is my professional name; I don't want the people in the supermarket where I work to know that I'm an artist."

Raymond started to say, "Do you really think…" then left unsaid "that would they find out." The dual identity gave Li an air of mystery—it was part of the enhanced experience Raymond was seeking.

"Shall we say that I'll stop by in two days, same time? I'll bring you your phone, and we'll work on planning your exhibitions."

# # #

Li resumed his place at the window, watching Raymond Chartrier's back until the man had turned onto the sidewalk and disappeared. He removed the painting from the closet, put it on his easel, then stood back and smiled. The tableau wasn't an exact copy of the Little Bacchanal; instead, it was how Li imagined Nicolas Poussin might have painted a similar scene featuring the infant Bacchus. Without all the equipment needed to fake a Poussin painting, it was more like a composition inspired by Poussin, done in his style. Li was pleased with the result; you could sense the joy in the little children and laugh at the infant Bacchus drinking grape juice. He'd outlined the remaining image—a tall satyr. Filling in that last figure was all that remained to complete his painting. After that, he'd hang the painting from a nail on the wall and take comfort from it at times of self-doubt.

He remembered doing two copies of *Baby Moses in the River*. He'd been proud of the result; he'd come close to approximating Poussin's technique and imagined that Poussin could have painted such a scene. Of course, Jacques Mornnais had removed the paintings as soon as they were completed; he treated Li and Wen as two robots calibrated to produce fakes and copies on demand. But the infant Bacchus tableau was his and his alone.

He cleared his mind and started to work on the satyr's form until the light had begun to fade. He left the painting on his easel and heated a bowl of noodles and vegetables.

CHAPTER FORTY-SEVEN

Lyon

BRUNO WISHED HE HADN'T GONE to dinner at Chez Blondie, wished he hadn't seen the red-haired cow and her friends. And the fucking painting, he wished that he hadn't seen that either. It reminded him of Jacques and of what the painters and the maid had done to him. But right now, he needed to focus on Father Paul.

The next morning, before returning to Toulouse, he took the funicular up to the Fourvière hill. He sat on one of the benches in the park outside the basilica, but instead of finding the view of the city below soothing, he felt agitated when he remembered that he'd met with the American here. The American who'd helped him to recover some of his memories. Which led him to replay the film of the fateful night in the château, until Jacques' voice intruded: *"I don't know how you got my number, but I'm sorry, Bruno Edremal is dead. If this is a joke, it's not funny. Good-bye."*

He needed to clear his mind, and he got up and started to walk briskly. Suddenly, he realized that he was walking past the Saint-Bernard Study Center, where he had last seen Father Paul. There'd been one other person in the house: an old priest, who had died of illness or old age, maybe both. His head started to ache; it felt like a pneumatic drill was piercing holes behind his eyes.

Bruno craved a coffee. In the past, it would have been a drink, but he was still repulsed by alcohol. He entered the first café on his route—it was at the bottom of the steep incline.

"A double espresso, please."

There was only one other customer at the bar, drinking a beer. Bruno smiled inwardly: that would have been him not so long ago. As the caffeine coursed through his system, he took a closer look around. He realized that it was the same café where he had stopped last January after he'd run out of the study center. And, incredibly, Bruno recognized the man drinking a beer: it was the delivery driver who had picked up the package at the study center. *The man must stop in here every morning*, he thought.

"Hey," he said, "weren't you the guy who found a dead priest last January?"

The delivery driver swallowed his beer, wiped his mouth with the back of his hand: "Yeah, that's me unless there was more than one dead priest."

"No great loss," grunted the man behind the bar, as he emptied the dishwasher.

"It was one shit day, I can tell you that. Had to drive to a shit town called Gaillac, broke down along the way."

"Gaillac?"

"Yeah, why, d'ya know it?"

"No, not really."

If Bruno needed any further confirmation that it *was* Father Paul that he'd seen in Gaillac, he just received it. He was anxious to return to Toulouse, even if he needed to wait until September to continue with his plan.

# # #

Trubenne

Eugene was stretched out in the hammock that hung between two oak trees. He looked up at the sliver of blue sky that peaked through the dark leaves, felt the gentle breeze that rustled those leaves ever so slightly, and concluded that he was bored. The long summer months spent with Alex — doing carpentry and painting in the château — that was all great, but he felt that he needed a project, a goal, something to test his wits and get the adrenaline coursing through his veins while he waited to find Jacques Mornnais and the secret of his birth parents.

He called Vital; the lawyer was out of breath; he'd been playing tennis.

"Hello Vital, it's Eugene Spector, Alexia's friend."

"Yes?" Vital waited to hear what that colorless man had on his mind.

"We've been thinking about your proposal, and I'd like to come up to Paris. You know, just a man-to-man meeting, I'm sure we can work things out, what do you say?"

Vital smiled. *At last, they're coming around. Alexia, her friend (what did he say his name was?), even Richard — they've finally realized the situation they were in.*

"That's an excellent idea, Mr...I'm sorry, I didn't catch your name?"

"No problem: Spector, Eugene Spector." Eugene was smiling as well.

They agreed that Eugene would call Vital in September and make an appointment to go up to Paris to meet with him. That just left Jacques Mornnais. *We're a team* Bruno had said to him. He would find Bruno in Toulouse, where he hoped to pick his troubled brain. Eugene felt better. He got up and took a walk through the vineyard.

CHAPTER FORTY-EIGHT

September 2011
Vitry-sur-Seine

ON AN EARLY SEPTEMBER MORNING, Li realized that summer was ending. The days had started to get shorter, and he could feel the change in the weather. The oppressive heat was gone, the days were crisper, and the nights had a touch of chill. But something was amiss: instead of experiencing that surge of energy he needed to complete the paintings for his exhibition, he felt the all too familiar lump of fear in his belly. What if his paintings were not good enough, what if Raymond Chartrier changed his mind?

He'd had similar worries all the time he worked for Jacques Mornnais; would his fakes and forgeries be good enough? What if he were found out? He knew that Jacques would not hesitate to throw him to the dogs. It was a year and a half since he and Wen had left Château d'Hélène. The passage of time had not removed the hard edges of his hatred of Jacques and his right-hand man Bruno, whose mere presence had been torture for the two painters.

Bruno. They had slipped him into the river—good riddance, he'd thought. He remembered their flight from the château; it hadn't been difficult, as they had so few possessions, but he'd made sure to take his sketchbook. Li would leaf through the drawings of the château and its surroundings, the strange and brooding beauty inspiring his current paintings. He picked up the sketchbook now, and as he ran his fingers around the edges of the pages, he felt a calm come over him, and his energy returned as he put his worries to the back of his mind.

Raymond Chartrier came by in the evening. He brought Li his new cell phone and some news about the exhibition.

"Our first show will be in Toulouse," he said. "Originally, we thought we'd start in Lyon and then organize exhibitions in Bordeaux and Marseille, but we have the chance to show your work in an extraordinary venue in Toulouse, so we'll use that city to launch you. What do you think?"

"Whatever you say."

Li had done a series of paintings of Château d'Hélène: in the sunshine, in the rain, under gray skies. And now he was working on a large canvas, with yet another vision of the château. Gone were the carefully tended lawns and sculpted hedges and shrubs. In their place was the wild vegetation of the surrounding area. It looked as if the château was fighting against being swallowed up by the tall trees and bushes.

"My goodness," said the engineer, "That's quite different from your other works. It's almost frightening."

"At times it could be a frightening place and…" Li stopped. He did not want to get into his past, and while he was grateful to Raymond Chartrier, he wished that he'd go away and let him get on with his painting.

"Well, I'll just leave your new phone here on the table. And not to worry, I took care of the paperwork. I'll call you to make our final arrangements."

Li had already turned back to his easel before Raymond was out the door.

# # #

The truck carrying Li's paintings drove into the courtyard of the offices of *Servientes Mundi* on Rue Ninau. All of the pictures except one were hung on the walls of the vast lobby. That last canvas was so large, and the weather so clement, that the organizers decided to place it in the courtyard. In no time, they had built a small wooden platform, and now the painting was positioned to face the street.

CHAPTER FORTY-NINE

Gaillac

THE FIRST OF SEPTEMBER FELL on a Thursday. Bruno imagined that the priests had returned from their retreat earlier in the week, but he gave it a few more days, just to be sure, before continuing with his plan.

Late one night the following week, he donned a black hoodie, slipped a mask around his neck, and loaded the posters into the van, along with a pot of glue and a brush. Once he arrived in Gaillac, rather than returning to the municipal billboard, he drove in circles until he found the *Salle des Fêtes,* a public building used by the inhabitants for events, meetings, receptions, and the like. It was constructed of pale-yellow stone, with large windows overlooking the parking lot. Bruno looked around and, reassured that he was alone, quickly unloaded his cargo. He swabbed the two spaces between three of the windows with glue, then stuck the posters onto the rough surface, the ghastly skeletons now in place to greet visitors to the building. He stepped back to admire his work and hurried back to the van, pleased with the result.

Next, he drove to the vicinity of the *Résidence* and parked a few blocks away. Carrying a poster, his glue, and his brush, he walked up the street that ran alongside the faded rose-brick building. A momentary urge to plaster the poster on the building's façade quickly receded: the danger of being seen and, worse yet, interrupted was too great. Not that gluing the poster onto the door in the wall on the side street was without peril, but that was a risk he was willing to take. He raised his mask—it was a puppy with its tongue hanging out— and pulled up the hood of his sweatshirt. He spread the glue over the door and waited as a car drove past. When the street was again empty, he slapped the last poster onto the door, turned on his heel, and walked back to the van, imagining the reactions to his night's labors.

# # #

It started when an old woman, her chest heaving under a blue and pink flowered dress, knocked on the door of the *Résidence.* In the cool of early morning, she'd been on her way to the Abbey when she saw…and here the novice, lost in the stream of words—scandalous, sacrilegious, poster, the end of the world— decided to walk around the corner to look for himself. His stomach clenched when he saw the abomination from earlier in the summer plastered on the garden door. He hurried back inside and alerted Father Joseph. The priest-in-residence had to see for himself, and joined by the residents, he followed the novice's footsteps. Standing before the poster, the group broke into the same incoherent blabber as the old woman. Still chattering, they retired to the meeting room; only Father Paul was silent, his eyes seeming to focus on a point beyond the room's walls.

The novice was tasked with removing the poster. Afterward, the handyman would be brought in to paint the door to remove all traces of the monstrosity. Once again, a prayer of purification would be recited. As it was early in the day, with a bit of luck, no one other than the old woman had walked past the garden door. The thought sent a wave of relief through the group. That was before the phone rang.

# # #

The *Salle des Fêtes* didn't have a permanent employee; if someone wanted to use the space, they went to the Mayor's office to make the arrangements. A couple had reserved the building for their wedding reception; they picked up the keys at the Mayor's office and went to take measurements and figure out how they would set things up for the big day. As they approached the building, the woman noticed the posters first: "What the fuck? Do you see that?"

"What?" asked the groom-to-be, his attention focused on singing along with Katy Perry.

His future wife pointed at the façade, "THAT."

He parked the car, got out to look closer, and laughed. "A bit early for Halloween, don't you think?"

"It's not funny, Gabriel. It's horrible."

"I dunno. It's funny, but some of our guests might not have the same reaction. I'll call the Mayor's office to let them know that they'll need to send someone to remove that example of artistic expression. But not before I take a picture of it."

Gabriel made his phone call and sent the photo to the Mayor. But he didn't stop there. The more he thought about it, the more he realized that the poster was some kind of sick joke, and it amused him so much that he shared it with his friends.

When the Mayor called the *Résidence*—he felt they needed to hear about the poster from him—he learned about the discovery on the garden door earlier that morning. Someone was intent on spreading disrespect and hatred, but who…and why? They wondered if the poster might turn up in other places in Gaillac; the Mayor would instruct his small staff to be on the alert. In fact, thanks to Gabriel, the whole town was aware of the posters; many were disappointed when no others appeared.

While Father Joseph and the Mayor continued to discuss the appearance of the posters, uttering the same phrases—as if the constant repetition would leach the reality out of the situation—Father Paul was sitting on the edge of his bed, gripped by anxiety. The posters' appearance only confirmed his suspicion that Bruno Edremal had set the scene. He trembled as he wondered what the man would do next, for he knew there would be a next time.

Trapped in Gaillac, he dared not share his suspicions with Father Joseph. That would mean bringing up why he'd come to live here—better to leave those stones unturned. All that was left was for him to pray that Bruno

Edremal would tire of this game. Father Paul unlocked the black wheelie bag, found the magazine he'd secreted there, and pushed his problems away. For now.

# # #

Something about the poster was bothering Father Joseph: the skeleton in the garden is clothed in a black robe with the obscene banana, and the photos are glued on the garden door and the *Salle des Fêtes.* What did they mean? To be sure, it was an insult to the church, particularly the priesthood, but why, and why now? Had the culprit been triggered by some recent event? He looked at the newspapers accumulated during their retreat and skimmed through the headlines. But nothing caught his attention. The retreat. It had gone smoothly—but why wouldn't it: a bunch of old men living out their last days in the comfort provided by the church. The faces passed before his eyes; he stopped at one: Father Paul, the newest arrival. He knew the man's history, knew why he'd been sent to Gaillac. Father Joseph found Father Paul's presence distasteful but couldn't argue with the hierarchy. He only hoped that the church had stopped its practice of protecting sexual predators like Father Paul. Another thought arose: could there be a link between the skeleton and Father Paul? Outside of a few in the administration, no one else knew that he'd been relocated to Gaillac, and why. And yet, what if someone else did know? He went to the chapel and prayed for divine guidance.

CHAPTER FIFTY

Rue des Arts, Toulouse

THE SAME DAY, ALEX AND Eugene climbed the stairway to Jackie's apartment. Jackie had sent the family's clothing and personal items back to the US, and the only sign that children had lived there were two pairs of worn sneakers strewn haphazardly in the hallway, as though the boys had taken off their shoes when they entered the apartment. After they unpacked, Alex set about watering the greenery on the balconies. She pointed to the building across the street:

"That's where he lives."

"Are you sure?"

"Yes, and I think I see him, look, he's walking up the street."

Eugene looked over Alex's shoulder.

"That's not him, it's just some beefy guy past his prime." He wrapped his arms around her, "Don't worry, I'm sure we'll run into our friend Bruno, but you've got to stop thinking about him all the time." Bruno was foremost in Eugene's thoughts, but he didn't think it would help if he shared his preoccupation with Alex.

"You're right," she said. "Let me show you around the city." They descended the ancient stairway, Eugene following Alex as she retraced the steps of her visit with Jackie, "Yes, it's beautiful" he said at appropriate moments.

"There's a lovely park nearby. We can buy some food and picnic there."

As they walked down Rue Ninau towards Le Grand Rond, they saw a poster in front of an imposing building, advertising the opening of an exhibition that evening of a painter called Ma Zhen.

"Let's come back this evening," said Alex, I'd love to see the inside of that building."

"Why not?" Eugene's interest in art had ended when he'd recovered the money his aunt had paid for the fake Nicolas Poussin painting, but Alex's mood seemed to have lightened, and he didn't want to spoil that.

# # #

Alex and Eugene picked their way through the crowd that had spilled out onto the sidewalk, sidestepping the animated conversations punctuated by drinks and cigarettes. Once in the courtyard, Alex let out a small gasp.

"What's the matter?"

"Look, it's Château d'Hélène, or should I say a nightmare vision of Château d'Hélène?"

Eugene had only been to the château once and hadn't spent much time admiring the façade, but he recognized the building immediately. It stood out against a dark red sky, as though trying to escape from the encroaching vegetation. Eugene stared at the painting; were there faces concealed in the elaborately worked leaves and tree trunks?

"Who is Ma Zhen," Alex whispered to Eugene. "Do you think he worked for Jacques as well?"

"No way to tell, let's go inside—that painting gives me goose bumps."

As they entered the building, Alex saw an Asian man in conversation with a couple, the woman was pointing at one of the paintings; *perhaps she's going to buy it* thought Alex. "That's Li. I only met him once, but I think that I recognize him," she told Eugene.

"If that's him, then I understand why he's calling himself Ma Zhen," chuckled Eugene.

"That's not funny, Eugene."

“Sorry, Alex, but he and his pal did throw Bruno into the river.”

“Yes, but they thought he was already dead.”

“So they say.”

“I’m thinking, shouldn’t we warn Li that Bruno might be living nearby?

“We’re not positive, and we might spoil the guy’s exhibition for nothing. I suggest that we finish up here and go be tourists and sit on a café terrace and watch the world go by.”

CHAPTER FIFTY-ONE

BRUNO WAS BACK IN TOULOUSE. He was on edge, thinking about his trip to Gaillac. Had the priests in the *Résidence* seen the poster? And what about the posters he'd glued on the façade of the *Salle des Fêtes?* Had word about them gotten around the town? And Father Paul, did he suspect that Bruno was behind the recent activity? He hoped so.

As Bruno walked down Rue Ninau, he saw the crowd on the sidewalk in front of *Servientes Mundi* and realized that they were there for the opening of an art exhibition. It would be an excellent opportunity to go inside, perhaps get some more information on the group.

He almost missed the painting in the courtyard; a group of people blocked his way as he headed toward the entrance. When he turned to avoid them, his eyes were drawn to the dark red flash of color. And then to the rendering of Château d'Hélène. Ma Zhen? It was the work of one of the fucking painters, Li or Wen.

Forgotten was his interest in *Servientes Mundi;* he went inside to look for Li or Wen, or both. Across the room a young woman was seated at a table—it seemed as though she was there to answer questions. As Bruno approached her, he saw a slightly built Asian man; his pulse quickened as he recognized Li's fragile silhouette. A portly man had his arm around Li's shoulders and was guiding him towards the table. The girl said something to them; Li smiled and turned his head to look at one of the paintings. Had she told him that it had been sold?

Li's smile froze when he locked eyes with a tall, muscular man. He grabbed the table as he felt his knees buckle under him.

"Are you all right?" asked Raymond Chartrier. "Come over and meet the collector who's just purchased one of your paintings."

But Li stood rooted in place; the only movement was a vein in his forehead that throbbed. Bruno walked up to him:

"Why hello there, Li. It's been a while, hasn't it? I see that you're busy right now, but we'll have to get together soon."

Bruno's familiar smirk crossed his lips as he walked away. On his way out he stopped to stare again at the painting in the courtyard. *Too bad Jacques' not here to see this painting: Li's made the château look like a haunted house. I'll bet he would not have been amused.*

# # #

Eugene took Alex's hand and led her out of the building. The paintings inside were nice enough, but not his cup of tea. *What is my cup of tea*, he wondered? *Just like the definition of pornography: I know it when I see it.* He looked over at the painting in the courtyard…and saw Bruno's broad back.

"Guess who's here, admiring the artwork? It's our friend Bruno, maybe you did see him after all!"

Eugene dropped Alex's hand and started to walk over to Bruno, but the big man had had enough of the exhibition and had disappeared before Eugene could reach him.

"No harm done, I'm sure our paths will cross, seeing as he lives across the street. I could use a drink, how about you?"

CHAPTER FIFTY-TWO

Toulouse

"YOU LOOK LIKE YOU NEED some fresh air," said Raymond, and he led Li out onto the street. The momentary elation Li had felt when Raymond told him that he'd made his first sale was gone. In its place cold terror gripped his intestines. He needed to find a toilet.

Alex and Eugene were seated on the terrace of a café further along Rue Ninou.

"That's quite a coincidence, wouldn't you say, seeing both Li and Bruno at the same time?" she asked.

"If you mean attaching meaning to two random events, then yes, it's a coincidence. And here's another random event, coming up the street."

"Li," called out Alex, "it's so nice to see you. You did a painting for me, do you remember? Won't you join us?"

The painter stared at the blonde woman and her companion, a puzzled look on his face.

"You did a copy of a painting for me — *Storm Over the Sea* — does that ring a bell?"

Li turned to Raymond, "Would you excuse me please, these are some old friends."

Before Raymond could speak, Li ran into the café. "I'll be back in a moment," he said over his shoulder. He came back a few minutes later. The pain in his stomach had lessened, but the terror that Bruno would come walking up the street remained: *I wonder if he would attack me in front of these people?*

"What are you drinking?" asked Eugene. "How about some nice, chilled rosé?"

"Yes, thank you." Li looked at Alex. He recalled her coming to see him on Rue Gagnée: "You asked me to copy the Daubigny, didn't you?"

"Yes, I did. And I must say, it was an excellent copy."

"Oh yeah," added Eugene, "A most excellent copy," and he chuckled, remembering how Alex had switched the fake Daubigny for the real one.

Li looked puzzled: was it some joke that he didn't understand? He let it pass.

Eugene continued: "We saw Bruno at your exhibition, that must have been a surprise for you." And waited. He could sense that Alex was about to speak and gently pressed his hand down on hers. The color drained from Li's face.

"You know Bruno?" he asked.

"We met him last year, in Lyon. No one really *knows* Bruno, he's more of an acquaintance."

Eugene saw that Li's hand was shaking as he reached for his glass of rosé. Li was right to be frightened. Bruno could come ambling down the street at any moment. "Toulouse is so noisy, don't you think? We're staying right up the street; why don't we go back to our apartment, it will be much quieter?" he said.

# # #

Alex opened one of the bottles of rosé that she had left to chill in the refrigerator and served the wine. Li brought the glass to his lips. His hands had stopped shaking, he felt safer now that he was off the street and in the apartment.

"I guess you heard what happened at the château..." He left the phrase hanging.

"Why don't you tell us?"

"There isn't that much to tell. When we brought our dinner dishes back to the kitchen, the maid—her name was Ella—she was kind of upset. Bruno was lying on the floor, she said he'd tried to rape her and then he collapsed. We thought he was dead and decided to get rid of the body. We didn't want the police coming around, asking questions."

He stared at the pale pink liquid, took a sip, and continued: "He was a very cruel man. And you see, we thought he was dead. So, what was the harm in throwing him in the river? I've had no regrets but my friend Wen, he saw it differently. He was so depressed that he returned to China. Now I don't know what to do. I've started to make a name for myself as Ma Zhen, but I might be safer back in China."

Talking about Bruno brought back other memories: Jacques' nastiness, his wife Mila's disdain, and the surliness of Jacques' driver Tarek. While Li unburdened himself, Eugene walked to the window. He saw Bruno return to the building across the street.

"I think that you'll be safe enough in Paris. It wouldn't be easy for Bruno to find you among ten million people. C'mon, let's walk you back to your hotel."

Toulouse's nightlife was in full swing. People spilled out onto the sidewalks to smoke, carrying their drinks with them. The noise was like a warm blanket on a cold night. It wrapped itself around Li and pushed away the thoughts of the time he had spent at the Château d'Hélène.

"Thank you," he said to Eugene and Alex when they reached his hotel. "You're right, of course. How could he find me, there are so many immigrants from Asia, and to people like Bruno we all look the same, don't we?"

# # #

"Do you really think that Li's not in any danger?"

They had stopped in Place Saint-Georges for a last drink, drawn by the bright lights that twinkled in the darkness.

"Yeah, he's probably okay, but I hope he stays under the radar."

"Well, why don't you try to talk to Bruno? You know, explain that Li thought he was dead?"

Eugene smiled, not a joyous smile, just an upturning of the corners of the mouth that reminded her of Jacques Mornnais. "It's not that simple, Alex. It doesn't sound like they did very much to see if Bruno really *was* dead, they were all too happy to throw him in the river and get rid of him. So, I doubt that our friend Bruno will be in a forgiving mood."

"Yes, but…"

"No buts here. Remember that Bruno helped me to get Jacques' files when we were at the château. He hadn't meant to, but that's how things worked out. And, I think Bruno has some idea of Jacques' whereabouts, and finding Jacques, that's my priority right now. Sorry, but Li will have to fend for himself."

"I guess," she said. If she sounded unconvinced, he didn't hear her. "I'm starting to feel chilly, let's go home."

As they were nearing their apartment, they saw Bruno coming from the opposite direction.

I thought he had gone home. What had he been up to, wondered Eugene. But before he could get close enough to call out to him, Bruno had walked into his building.

"I'll try to catch him tomorrow."

Alex said nothing. She just wanted to get into bed. The day that had started out so well had gone south.

CHAPTER FIFTY-THREE

THE LATE-NIGHT REVELERS STAGGERED up Rue des Arts. They laughed as they urinated in front of chic boutiques, and their laughter reverberated as they rolled garbage bins down the narrow street.

But this time, Bruno didn't hear the noise. Until today, he'd been focused on finding Father Paul. But seeing the mural in the red-haired cow's restaurant had pulled his thoughts back to Château d'Hélène. Bruno again saw himself coming back into the château's dining room to find the maid Ella going through his jacket pockets. She'd run into the kitchen, he followed her, ready to give her the beating she deserved—and then he'd blacked out. He must have regained consciousness after that, for he remembered the noise his body made as he was dragged out of the kitchen, pulled down the gravel path and rolled into the river. Bruno shivered, thinking of the plunge into the icy river, how he'd clawed his way up the muddy riverbank and crawled to the hut nearby. It was all because of those fucking painters and the fucking maid.

And now, he'd seen Li, and he couldn't get him out of his mind. The painter had been with some fat guy — he was probably his dealer. Bruno had returned to the exhibition later that evening, trying to find out more about Li, but the place was closed.

A police siren wailed, interrupting his thoughts. Now he heard the noise from the street. Someone must have called the cops, and for once they were going to do something about the damn noise. It was about time.

The cops. No one had ever called them to complain about Father Paul. It was too late now, and he was going to take care of the priest himself. But first, there was the painter. *I'm not going to let that little fucker get away.*

# # #

The next morning, Bruno stood in front of the full-length mirror: the image was rough and needed work. If he was going to pretend to be a collector, then he needed to look the part. He showered, donned a shirt and jeans that had come back from the dry cleaners, put on a pair of Chelsea boots, went downstairs and found a barber to trim his hair and his three-day beard. He'd done this sort of work for Jacques—pretending to be a disgruntled employee or a consultant or even a collector, come to think of it—and he slipped right into his new role. When he wasn't smirking or snarling, Bruno was an attractive man, except that there was something unsettling about his eyes. Even when he looked straight at you, his thoughts seemed to be elsewhere.

As Bruno neared the *Serviatis Mundi* courtyard, Raymond Chartrier climbed into a van, and by the time Bruno entered the yard, the van had pulled out into the street. He walked past Li's rendering of the Château d'Hélène and went inside, intent on finding out how to contact the painter that called himself Ma Zhen.

Bruno walked around the exhibition, studying the paintings until he found what he was looking for. It was a tableau with the château in the background; a lone bird perched on a naked tree branch in the foreground. He felt that the bird was preparing to fly away. There were two labels on the frame: a white one with the number 27, and next to it, a round red sticker.

A woman sat behind a table at the back of the room. To one side of her there was a pile of papers, she looked at each document, wrote on a notepad, and transferred the page to another stack. She wore a sleeveless black top; it was low-cut and presented a view of her ample cleavage. She looked up as she felt Bruno approach.

"May I help you?"

"I hope so. I see that there's a red sticker on number 27. I guess that means that it's been sold?"

The woman turned to consult a list at the edge of the table.

"Yes, that's right. Why, are you interested in that painting?"

"Yes, I am."

"Why don't you take another look around? The artist has done several views of the château as seen through the forest."

"I already have. No, that's the painting that I want. I'd like to talk with the artist, see if he'd do another one like that for me."

"Well, you'd have to talk to Mr. Chartrier, he's the man who organized this exhibition, but I'm afraid he's left to return to Paris."

"And how might I reach Mr. Chartrier?" He had stepped closer, placed his hands on the table and leaned towards her. She took in his Rolex at the same time as she felt him staring at her exposed breasts. It wasn't the lustful gaze that she was used to and enjoyed, but rather a neutral examination of her body, as though he was contemplating a park bench or a tree trunk. Bruno had not moved, but she had a sudden feeling of danger. She rose, pulling on her black top to try to cover herself.

"I'll get you one of his cards, he left them in the office, I'll be right back."

She walked quickly to a door on the opposite side of the room. As soon as her back was turned, Bruno came around to the other side of the table and pushed the pile of papers to get a better look. If the woman came back, he'd say sorry, that he was looking for the price list. It was as if an electric current had passed through his body when he saw the bill from a cell phone provider: the user's name was Ma Zhen. With the pickpocket's deft touch, he slipped the document off the table and into his jacket pocket.

He smiled at the woman as she returned to the table. She handed Bruno Raymond Chartier's business card, her outstretched hand keeping the maximum distance between them.

Bruno took no notice of the scarf she had draped around her neck, to cover the tops of her breasts. He had gotten what he'd come for, and she had ceased to exist.

"Thanks," he said, looking through her.

He went to the café across the street and took the cell phone bill out of his pocket: Li was living in Vitry-sur-Seine, a city to the south of Paris, full of immigrants, some legal, some not. *Lucky day for me—otherwise, I never would have found the fucker.*

CHAPTER FIFTY-FOUR

Vitry-sur-Seine

BRUNO HAD DRIVEN TO PARIS and checked into a cheap tourist hotel near Gare du Nord. The next morning the sky was turning from dark to pale gray when he rose and headed to the town of Vitry-sur-Seine. He looked for a parking place a few doors up from Li's house, although he doubted that Li would see him through the car's tinted windows.

At seven-thirty a.m., Li left the house. He had kept his day job at the supermarket and hurried to the bus stop. Bruno stayed in the car. His first impulse had been to follow Li, but then he thought better of it; the painter might notice him among the black, brown, and yellow faces, he might panic and do something stupid. No, Bruno had another plan.

He waited for half an hour, and when Li didn't return, he guessed that he'd gone off to work. Bruno entered the house and climbed the worn stairway to Ma Zhen's apartment. He pulled a set of keys out of his pocket and let himself in. The smell hit him first. It was a mixture of cooking oil, onion and garlic, along with the odor of paint and turpentine. *How could the man live like that?*

Bruno opened a window to relieve his nausea, taking deep breaths of fresher air, and looked around the room. A small table was crammed with Li's palette, paints and brushes, rags, and various cans and bottles. At the end of the table lay Raymond Chartrier's business card and a large envelope that had been torn open. He skimmed the contents: it was Li's contract with Raymond.

Then he saw the painting on the easel. Bruno's face stared back at him from the large canvas. Li had captured the empty, foreboding gaze, the sensual mouth twisted into a cruel sneer. But the painting still needed work. For the background, Li had sketched in the river. *Was the river rising or falling,* he wondered. *Is Li trying to kill me once again?*

Continuing his examination of the room, Bruno slid open the closet door. In one corner was a pile of dirty laundry; a few articles of clothing hanging on wire hangers did not obscure the painting leaning against the closet's back wall. Bruno removed his portrait from the easel and replaced it with the painting from the closet. The tableau was unlike the paintings he had seen at the exhibition; instead, it reminded him of the fake Poussins Li had done for Jacques. He looked more closely, his gaze taking in the frolicking children, an infant drinking something that looked like wine or juice, the satyr…The satyr, a figure in the background, was unfinished; Li had outlined the figure, including ears, horns, and tail, but the image was incomplete.

As Bruno stared at the painting—asking himself *what does this mean, what's the story*—the same feeling he'd experienced at the Centre d'Etudes Saint-Bernard came over him, and he suddenly felt anxious to leave the small, foul-smelling room. He returned the painting to the closet and replaced the portrait on the easel. He closed the window, took another look at the portrait, locked the door, and went downstairs to sit in his car and wait for Li. Eyes shut, he fell asleep. In his dream, the mouth in the portrait spoke to him, and when he awoke an hour later, he knew what he needed to do. He got out of his car, walked in the neighborhood, ate a sandwich, walked some more, rehearsed his plan, then returned to his car to wait for the painter.

CHAPTER FIFTY-FIVE

LI RETURNED IN THE LATE afternoon. It was the lightest he had felt since the night they had thrown Bruno into the river. Raymond had called to say that the exhibition had been a success. They had sold several paintings, and a collector had come by asking if Li could do a special commission for him.

The first thing he did when he entered his room was to air the place out. Something was unsettling. Was it the odor—he couldn't say. He looked around the room; everything was as he had left it and yet he couldn't shake the queasiness in his midsection. He stood at the window, looked up at the still cloudless blue sky, and decided to take a walk along the river Seine, to shake the uncomfortable feeling.

# # #

Bruno had been half dozing, but he sat up with a start when he saw the movement at the window. He had planned to confront Li when the painter came home, but he changed his plans when he saw Li walking out of the building.

As Li headed up the street, Bruno got out of the car and keeping a safe distance, followed him. *Where is he going* wondered Bruno, and then a dull grey-blue ribbon came into view. It was the Seine.

Bruno hung back as he waited for Li to cross the busy thoroughfare that ran along the river below. He watched him walk along the sidewalk until he came to the steps leading down to the river. The painter continued along the waterfront. It was deserted, except for a few old men who stood at the water's edge, fishing. They paid no attention to Li as he stretched out on an unoccupied bench. Was it his job in the supermarket that had tired him out, or was it the effort he had put into preparing the paintings for his exhibition? Whatever it was, he soon fell asleep as the late summer sun dropped lower on the horizon.

The sun had now set, the fishermen returned home, and a chill breeze blew off the river. Li opened his eyes; there was a figure sitting at the end of the bench. He blinked rapidly and the form turned to look at him.

"Hello there, Li, or should I say, Ma Zhen? It looks like we meet again, small world, isn't it?"

Li looked for someone to call out to, but the waterfront was empty. As he sat up, Bruno sprang to his feet and put his hands on Li's thin shoulders.

"Sit still, we're going to have a conversation." It was the menacing voice Li had heard so often at the château. His heart started to beat so rapidly—as if it would burst through his chest—and he struggled to breathe.

"What I don't understand is why did you do it? Okay, you and your buddy didn't like me, hated me, maybe, but why kill me?" Li was too terrified to see the irony in Jacques' henchman complaining that they had tried to kill him.

"I'm sorry," his voice cracked, "But we thought you were already dead. And besides, you tried to rape Ella."

"I didn't touch the fucking maid," he snarled. "But even if I did, what's it to you?" The space behind his eyes started to throb. "Anyway, I'm tired of talking. Get up. You're going to go for a swim, just like I did. And at least you're not half dead the way I was."

While Bruno talked, Li looked around desperately, but there was no sign of life on the waterfront. The noise of the traffic on the street above would drown out any call for help. Bruno, holding his shoulders in a vise-like grip, pushed Li towards the edge of the walk and into the river.

"So long," said Bruno. He stood on the quay and watched Li struggle to keep his head above the water. Then, overcoming the urge to leave Li to drown, he extended a hand. Li gripped the outstretched fingers, and Bruno pulled him out of the river. The painter lay on the pavement, gasping for breath. The streetlights had come on, and in the distance, Bruno saw two forms walking along the quay. As they approached, Bruno leaned over Li, as though to comfort him, whispering, “Don’t say a word, or I’ll throw you back in for good.” The men stopped to look—do you need help? Is everything OK; thanks, but he’s OK; he just had a bit of a fright. Thanks, though.

Then Bruno pulled Li to his feet. “I’ll take you home now.”

CHAPTER FIFTY-SIX

EXHAUSTED FROM HIS NEAR-DEATH dunk in the river, Li leaned heavily against Bruno as they walked back to Li's dwelling. Bruno, not taking any chances, kept his arm wrapped tightly around Li's shoulders; a casual observer might think that the bigger man was doing no more than accompanying his companion home after one drink too many.

Li's keys had been clipped onto his belt, and when they reached the landing, although his hands were still shaking, he could open the door. Inside, Bruno pushed him onto the bed, then sat at the table, his legs spread akimbo, hands on his thighs, his empty eyes fixed on the painter. He watched as Li breathed heavily, the movement of his chest visible under his damp tee shirt; the man's eyes were closed as if to shut out the reality of his situation.

A door slammed somewhere in the building. The noise seemed to startle Bruno. He rose, walked to the closet, removed the painting leaning against the wall, and carried it to the easel. He smirked as he threw the portrait on the floor and placed the tableau on the easel.

"Get up," he said to Li, and before the painter had time to react, Bruno pulled him to his feet and dragged him across the room to stand in front of the easel. "You're gonna do some painting for me, just like you did for Jacques." And he told Li what he wanted him to do.

Li hesitated as Bruno gave his instructions, for he realized that Bruno intended to take the painting away. Not just take it away but destroy its beauty. Bruno, impatient now, snarled, "Do it now, or I'll fix you so you won't ever paint again."

It took Li an hour to comply with Bruno's request. When he was done, Bruno took the painting and leaned it against the door, careful not to disturb the wet paint. Now, he picked up the portrait and replaced it on the easel.

The unforgiving face stared at him, locked him in its gaze. A thousand hammers pounded in his head. Overcome with rage, he seized a kitchen knife; he no longer saw the painting but Li himself. One slash, another, and another, until the painting was destroyed. When he was done, bits of paint-covered cloth were strewn over the floor like wilted flower petals; one eye looked at him from a canvas ribbon hanging from the stretcher bar.

Bruno picked up the tableau with the children and left the room. He didn't bother to close the door.

# # #

Li was alone now. Bruno had forced him to ruin his precious painting of the infant Bacchus, and he felt an emptiness in the pit of his stomach—all the work and love he'd put into the painting had gone out the door. He gazed around the room and contemplated the defaced painting, the tattered scraps of the portrait of the man who was the source of his misery. His body shook with sobs; he had lost so many of life's battles.

When he calmed down, he got up and made himself a pot of tea. He didn't belong in Europe; that was clear. Wen had been right: now he, too, had no choice but to return to China. There was no reason that he could not continue to paint there. Li looked again at the remains of the portrait: an ominous eye hanging in space. He had been truthful when he told Bruno that he was sorry about throwing him in the river, but as he stared at the eye, he thought that, given another chance, he'd be happy to put an end to that walking mass of cruelty.

CHAPTER FIFTY-SEVEN

Rue des Arts, Toulouse

BRUNO HAD BOUGHT A ROLL of brown paper and wrapped up the painting of the infant Bacchus. He used a black Sharpie pen to print a message smack in the center of the package, his familiar smirk frozen on his face. He'd called his friends in Marseille to ask if they could do him another small favor: he needed their driver to deliver a package for him. The destination was in Gaillac, it shouldn't take very long to run the errand. Bruno didn't want the van to pull up in front of his building on Rue des Arts—you could never tell when some nosy person would notice things best left unseen. He set out for the meeting place in the Côte Pavé neighborhood. It was not a short walk, and he had time to review his plan and savor the hoped-for outcome.

The driver pulled up just as Bruno arrived at number 17, Rue du Sergent-Vigné. As he had many times when working for Jacques, Bruno spit out his instructions: "Look, this is very simple; just do exactly as I say. You drive to Gaillac and park a few blocks behind the Abbey. That's important. No one should see the van. Take this package to the *Résidence* on the square in front of the Abbey. Got it so far? Good. Ring the bell. When they open the door, hand them the package and say it's for Father Paul. If they ask you any questions, say you don't know. Someone gave you the package and told you to deliver it. Don't get into a discussion. Leave the package and walk away. You OK with that?"

Do you think I'm stupid or something? That was the expression on the driver's face. But he simply replied, "Yeah, all good."

# # #

Things turned out to be less than all good. First, there was the problem of finding a parking place near the *Résidence* but not too close. Bruno had made it sound like that was no big deal, but it seemed as if everyone in Gaillac had parked in the town center. The driver had no choice but to leave the van closer to the outskirts, meaning he'd have to walk a kilometer or so, carrying the bulky package. He felt that all eyes were on him as he made his way, passing people returning from work or doing their end-of-the-day grocery shopping. Anxious to be done, he quickened his pace and soon approached the *Résidence,* its faded bricks glowing in the early evening sunlight.

He rang the bell, heard it echoing inside, and waited. What the fuck, was anyone there? The door opened as he lifted his hand to ring the bell again. The first thing the driver saw was a protruding Adam's apple, then the blemishes on the neck and cheeks, and finally the face. *Looks kinda young to be a priest, but that's not my problem.*

"Yes?" *He seems edgy, better to get this over with and get outta here.* He thrust the package towards the novice, "Here, this is for Father Paul." But instead of taking the package, the novice took a step backward, "I don't know if I can accept that."

"Whatdya mean? Here, take it. I'm just the delivery man."

"What I mean is, who sent the package?"

"I dunno. Like I said, I'm just the deliverer."

Don't get into a discussion. Leave the package and walk away. Seeing as how the man at the door did indeed seem in the mood to have a conversation, the driver shoved the package through the opening, turned on his heel, and strode swiftly back to where he'd parked the van.

The novice stood motionless. He watched the delivery man disappear, then picked up the package, holding it gingerly, and took it inside to show Father Joseph. He hoped he would not be angry with him.

CHAPTER FIFTY-EIGHT

Gaillac

FATHER JOSEPH LOOKED ONCE MORE at the package that leaned against the far wall of his office. He'd read the message—printed in neat block letters: *For Father Paul, In Remembrance.* Then he closed his eyes and gathered his thoughts.

First, he had questioned the novice, but the boy was truly useless. His description of the delivery man—medium height, dark hair, neither long nor short, wearing jeans and a white tee-shirt—could fit half the men in Gaillac. And although the novice denied it, he seemed frightened. But of what? Next, Father Joseph thought about the abomination in the garden and the posters that had appeared soon after. It was a vile image of a sinful priest mocking the clergy.

He looked at the package once more. Perhaps he shouldn't open it, just destroy it and forget about the whole business. But curiosity got the better of him, and he carefully removed the wrapping, leaving the message intact. His glance fell first on the frolicking infants, then on the infant Bacchus, and lastly on the satyr, dressed in a priest's garb, its sex large and erect. Staring at the painting, the blood rose to his cheeks, and his breath got caught in his throat; he made the sign of the cross and draped the brown paper over the painting. This time, Father Joseph didn't have to ask himself what it meant. Instead, he asked himself what needed to be done. The answer was not long in coming. And when it did, he rang a bell on his desk to call the novice and asked him to tell Father Paul that he'd like to see him.

# # #

Father Paul had a constant pain in his belly. At first, he thought it might be due to the meals they served in the *Résidence,* except that no one else complained about the food. While his health had started to deteriorate in Lyon—a growing shortness of breath, stiffness in his joints—things had gotten worse since his arrival in Gaillac. Recently, he had trouble holding on to his thoughts, the images melting into each other until a piercing stab in his abdomen brought him back to the present. And now, Father Joseph had asked to see him; hopefully, it was not to send him away to yet another hiding place.

Taking his first steps into Father Joseph's office, Father Paul didn't notice the object covered in brown paper leaning against the wall. Instead, he stood staring into the nothingness until the priest-in-residence asked him to be seated, then spoke:

"I want to show you something." He approached the wall and pointed to the covering: "This was delivered today; as you can see, it's marked 'For Father Paul, In Remembrance.' Do you have any idea who could be sending you gifts?"

Father Paul felt a stab of pain in his midsection and shook his head, "No," he murmured, "I have no idea."

"Actually, I would not call it a gift. Rather, a slap in the face," said Father Joseph, removing the brown paper and exposing the painting. "Come closer and have a look."

Doubled over in pain, Father Paul approached the painting, his gaze transfixed by the frolicking cherubs and the villainous satyr. A short intake of breath stifled any words caught in his throat.

"If we ignore the menacing figure of the satyr, it's a beautiful painting, wouldn't you agree? I don't know much about art, but the children are so lovingly rendered in what looks to be some sort of mythological scene. It's as though the artist painted a pastoral scene and then had second thoughts and inserted the menacing figure of the satyr in a priest's robe. I'm wondering why someone would send that to you…"

"I, I don't know," stammered Father Paul. *It could only be Bruno Edremal, but better to say nothing.* Still unable to stand erect, he shuffled back to his chair.

"How are you feeling; you seem unwell."

"Oh, it's nothing, just an upset stomach."

"Still, I think it needs looking after. I'll make the necessary arrangements and let you know."

The priest-in-residence stood up; the meeting was over.

# # #

After the door closed behind Father Paul, Father Joseph crossed the room to examine the painting more closely. As he'd told Father Paul, he didn't know much about art, but he had a keen sense of observation. The more that he looked at the painting, the more he felt that something was not right, but what was it? He could sense the robustness of the infants, admire the play of light on their firm bodies, and feel how they moved. He could feel the love and attention the adults dispensed to the infants. No, it was the evil satyr; he didn't belong in the tableau. He wondered if the satyr could be removed; if so, he'd be pleased to hang the painting on the walls of the *Résidence.* He remembered a non-profit foundation in Toulouse that had ties to the church; perhaps they would know someone in that city who could help him. He made a note to call *Servientes Mundi* when he had a free moment.

CHAPTER FIFTY-NINE

THE HOLIDAY IN TOULOUSE PASSED by quickly. When Eugene and Alex weren't spending their time out of doors—visiting monuments, sunning themselves on café terraces or dining outside—they were back at the apartment, making love. Eugene felt relieved that he'd told Alex about his quest to discover the identities of his birth parents—as he grew older, it had become more important to him.

His thoughts were focused on the folder in the box labeled "Ukraine;" it was among the files he had taken from the Château d'Hélène. There had been a piece of paper, torn out of an address book, with Viktor Kornarski's name and a phone number. Of course, he'd tried the number, but all he got was a busy signal. To learn more, he needed to find Jacques Mornnais.

But Jacques Mornnais had vanished. Eugene's only hope was that a thought would bubble up from Bruno's memory that could lead him to Jacques. Bruno: they had tried to keep an eye on the building across the street from their apartment, but for the moment, Bruno had disappeared as well.

They drove back to Trubenne in the bittersweet sunshine of summer transitioning to autumn. It hadn't rained much, and spring's vibrant palette of every shade of green had faded or turned yellow. When she saw other vineyards along the road, Alex talked about the grape vines they had planted at Trubenne last spring. It would be several years before they could start to produce good wine, but she was excited as she envisioned the future.

She reached into her bag and pulled out her cell phone to call Marie-Agnès—she hadn't spoken with her friend since they had left for Toulouse — and saw that her battery was at zero.

"Oh shit. It was so nice to disconnect that I completely forgot to charge my phone."

She plugged the charger into the dashboard, and several minutes later the phone beeped. Alex frowned as she read the message from Vital Vesla de Trubenne: "My dear cousin, I look forward to my meeting in September with your friend Eugene. VVdT."

"Are you going to meet Vital? How did that happen? And why didn't you tell me?" *Was Eugene up to his old tricks of keeping things to himself? At least he looks ashamed.*

'I'm sorry, Alex. I was feeling bored one afternoon and I called Vital and proposed to come up to Paris to meet with him. Don't take this the wrong way, but I don't think he believed you when you said that we'd fight him in court. He's the kind of man who has no respect for women, so he didn't take you seriously. Unfortunately, he needs to hear those words from a man. I should have told you, but it slipped my mind."

Alex stared straight ahead, seemingly torn between wanting to believe Eugene and feeling annoyed with him.

Eugene talked over the wall of silence. "If it's okay with you, I'll call Vital when we get back to Trubenne, make an appointment to see him, and set things straight."

"And what does that mean?"

"Like I said, I don't think he believed you when you said that we'd fight him in court. I intend to convince him that it would be best to drop any idea of guardianship or getting shares in Trubenne.

Alex shrugged, irritated that Vital didn't take her seriously, but maybe Eugene was right. Anyway, what did they have to lose? If Vital wanted to go to court, she was ready.

# # #

Paris

Eugene had called Vital. He had heard the smile in the lawyer's voice. He was sure that Vital thought that they were coming around to his point of view. *Let him dream a little longer.*

A few days later Alex drove Eugene to the train station in Nîmes where he boarded the fast train to Paris. He hadn't noticed it before, but making his way through Gare de Lyon, Eugene was struck by the sea of pale, unsmiling faces: people who pedaled furiously on the treadmills of their lives. *Has life in the south of France changed me*, he wondered. He didn't think so; he'd never stepped on to the treadmill, to begin with.

He checked into the same small tourist hotel near Avenue de Wagram. *I've got to watch out. I'm becoming a creature of habit.* Eugene arrived at Vital's office at nine fifty-five a.m., in time for his ten o'clock appointment. Vital stepped out to greet him twenty minutes later. He hadn't been with a client or anyone else, and Eugene understood that making him wait was nothing more than a cheap tactic to try to get on his nerves.

"Good morning, Eugene."

Vital sat down behind the safety of his desk, and smiled as he asked, "How can I help you?" He looked to be relishing the moment, perhaps waiting for Eugene to propose giving him a share in the house at Trubenne. His joy was short-lived. Eugene furrowed his brow. He had placed a cheap faux-leather document case on the chair beside him—he'd bought the case at an outdoor market in Nîmes. He reached for the folder and said, "It's more a question of how I can help you, I think."

Vital crossed his arms across his chest. It seemed that the conversation was not going as he had anticipated. "Excuse me, what's that supposed to mean?"

"Someone, I guess you could call him a sort of friend of the family, brought these photos over to the house. Of course, between us, it's not a big deal, but you can imagine how shocked Richard and Alexia were. Especially, Alexia, she went apeshit, if you'll excuse my language."

Eugene had placed three glossy black and white photos on Vital's desk. In the first photo, the photographer had caught Vital snorting a line of coke.

In the second, he was naked, entwined with two women on a large, heart-shaped bed. And in the third, he was part of a foursome; a lot was going on, and they seemed to be enjoying themselves.

Vital's breath came in short gasps; "Where did you get these?" he squeaked.

"I told you, a friend of the family came by, he was, you know, concerned."

Vital tried to regain control of the exchange: "Concerned about what, exactly?"

"Well, if these photos came out, you know, with internet and everything, it wouldn't do much for your reputation, at least not among those who count." Eugene paused, and then continued, "I mean, imagine if these came out during the guardianship proceeding."

"You're trying to blackmail me," sputtered Vital.

"Not really, I'm just trying to look out for your interests." Eugene rose: "I don't want to take any more of your time." He pointed to the photos: "I'll leave these with you, we have others.

CHAPTER SIXTY

Paris

WITHOUT MEANING TO, JACQUES MORNNAIS had been helpful. When he was back in Washington, Eugene had looked for a file with the lawyer's name on it among the documents that he'd stolen from Jacques, and he had found a folder marked VVdT. Inside there were six photos; Eugene had chosen the three that looked the most compromising. Travis had come up empty-handed on the lawyer, but in the end, his help had not been necessary.

Eugene was pleased with the way his meeting with Vital had gone. He had pegged Vital as a bully, and like all bullies, the man would back down at the first sign of resistance. It was now late morning, and Eugene walked over to Café Carré for an early lunch. He remembered the times he and Alex had met here. He thought about how she had borrowed Nathalie Martin's identity when she went to work for Jacques Mornnais. He remembered too how she had arranged for him to meet Merv Peters, which had eventually led to Jacques Mornnais' refunding the money his aunt had paid for the counterfeit Nicolas Poussin painting.

Things always seemed to be coming back to Jacques Mornnais. Eugene knew that Alex wanted nothing more to do with the man, but he also knew that she understood his need to discover the truth about what had happened in Ukraine so many years ago.

Today's special was mussels in a wine and garlic sauce. Eugene's love of garlic had not abated, but he avoided garlic-spiced food when he was with Alex; she'd made clear her displeasure with the smell. But today Alex was hundreds of kilometers away and he indulged himself and enjoyed his meal. Afterward, he took a taxi to the Tino Rossi Garden along the Seine and walked to the Guy de Rougemont sculpture. The ensemble of colorful cylinders was the place where he met Kenneth Petit, his contact in the French security services.

Eugene was not one to pile on stress or worry. He'd been telling himself to just do it long before the Nike ad appeared in 1988. When he went to meet Kenneth Petit, he wasn't concerned with the outcome of the encounter; either Kenneth would provide the information Eugene was seeking, or if not, there would probably be a clue in what he left unsaid.

Kenneth was sitting on a nearby bench, smoking a cigarette when Eugene arrived and sat down next to him. This time, Eugene had chosen to place the envelope with his snapshots in *Humanité,* the French Communist party's newspaper.

"It's just the President's wife with a friend," he said. "No big deal, but if we have the photos, I'll bet others do too? Just thought you might want to know." The photos had come from Jacques Mornnais' files.

Kenneth picked up the newspaper, folded it and slipped it into an inner pocket of his jacket. "So, how are things?" he asked, waiting to see what Eugene wanted in return.

"Pretty good, no complaints. I was wondering, though. Still no news on our friend Jacques Mornnais? He seems to have disappeared." His chewing gum had lost its flavor, and he swallowed it.

"Yeah, hasn't he?"

"Is he gone for good?"

"It depends on what you mean by 'gone for good.'"

"I mean is he dead or alive?"

"I didn't say he was dead. Let's say he's gone for good. That should tell you everything you need to know."

"I don't suppose you can tell me where he is?"

Kenneth Petit looked straight ahead. “You’re right.”

“I just want to talk to him.”

Kenneth Petit turned to face his friend, “Get over it, Eugene. He’s gone. *Raison d’état.* I’m sure you can get that.”

He stood up and patted his jacket, “Thanks for this, now I owe you one.”

You’ve already told me what I need to know. Eugene popped another stick of gum into his mouth, took a taxi back to his hotel, and hurried to catch the train to the south.

CHAPTER SIXTY-ONE

Gaillac

"I DID AS YOU SAID," the driver told him. Bruno nodded, grunted, "Thanks," and focused on his next step. He would go to the *Résidence Saint-Michel* and ask to see Father Paul, then retreat before the priest appeared. *Let him wonder if it's me, that ought to mess his head up.*

When he got to Gaillac, Bruno could see signs of life at the *Résidence.* Some windows were open, and the drapes were drawn back to let in the sweet autumn air. A young novice—different from the one who'd viewed the scene in the garden— came to the door when Bruno rang the bell. This one had dark rings under his eyes; his nose was peeling, a remnant of the retreat. He wore a black robe that was a size too small, and his bony wrists hung from the robe's sleeves like two thin bird's claws.

"Yes," he said.

"I've come to visit my uncle—Father Paul—I understand he's living here now."

"Oh, yes, Father Paul. He's not here now."

Bruno trembled, "What do you mean, he's not here now?"

"He left yesterday. That's all I know. Perhaps you should talk to Father Joseph, he's the priest-in-residence."

For a long moment, Bruno didn't see the novice's face; the familiar black curtain had descended, blocking his view. When the curtain rose, he saw the novice staring at him.

"Well, if that's all..." the young man began to say, but Bruno had already turned on his heel and started to walk away.

Fuck. The priest had managed to slip away once again. Where had he gone? And how was Bruno going to find him this time? He gunned the motorcycle; a tight knot of anger and disappointment grew in his midsection as he realized that his plans had gone off the rails.

# # #

Father Joseph was seated at his desk when the young novice knocked on the door. "A man just came by, asking to see Father Paul. Said he was his nephew. I told him Father Paul was no longer here, but he walked away when I asked if the man wanted to see you."

"I see. What did he look like?"

"A big guy, he wore a black sweatshirt and jeans. Looked a bit like an old rugby player."

"And his name, what was his name?"

"He didn't say. Just that he was Father Paul's nephew."

Was this the same man who'd come to the *Centre d'Etudes Saint-Bernard* in Lyon? If it was, how had he found Father Paul here in Gaillac? At least the problematic priest was now hidden safely away, or so Father Joseph hoped.

Father Joseph's gaze shifted to the painting, once again covered by brown paper, that leaned against the wall. Ah yes, he'd meant to deal with the painting; better do it now. He called *Servientes Mundi*: someone had gifted the *Résidence* a painting, but it was damaged. Did they know anyone in Toulouse who could restore the tableau?

The woman who answered the phone—the one with the *poitrine généreuse*—looked up at the exhibition. There were spaces on the wall; the paintings had sold well. She remembered the artist, a slightly built Asian man.

"I'll see what I can do," she told the caller and contacted

Raymond Chartrier.

"There's a home for retired priests not far from here. They have a painting that needs to be restored, and I thought of Ma Zhen; do you think he could be interested?"

Raymond was enjoying his new-found profession as an art impresario. Li's paintings—or should he say, Ma Zhen—had sold beyond his expectations, and Raymond was looking forward to staging other exhibitions. For that, he'd already asked Ma Zhen to provide new paintings. Throwing an extra bit of work his way could only help the artist's bank account; perhaps the man could even stop unloading crates in the supermarket. Raymond would call the painter this evening when he returned from work.

CHAPTER SIXTY-TWO

Vitry-sur-Seine

EVERY EVENING, AS HE RETURNED home, Li thought about Bruno: would his nemesis show up again at his apartment? Once again, he wondered if he shouldn't return to China as Wen had done. On the one hand, Raymond Chartrier had told him that the exhibition in Toulouse had been a success and that soon there would be other opportunities. But he could not shake the feeling that he'd not seen Bruno for the last time, and that frightened him and made him want to go halfway around the world to calm his nerves.

His cell phone—the one that Raymond had purchased for him—rang. A shiver ran up his spine; he tried to remember who he'd given his phone number to, and then Li breathed a sigh of relief when he saw Raymond's name on the screen.

"Hello, Li!"

"Ye..yes, hello Raymond," curious to know why Raymond was calling him, as they'd only spoken a few days ago. He'd already asked Li if he could provide more paintings as the people at Extra-Muros Culture wanted to organize another exhibition, so what could it be now?

"I have an interesting project for you; you could make some extra money, and..." Raymond paused before continuing. "I would not expect any commission."

"Yes," said Li. For the moment, it seemed that his vocabulary had been reduced to a single word.

"The people from *Servientes Mundi* called me. Remember, they're the ones hosting your exhibition in Toulouse. Anyhow, one of their connections—it's a home for retired clergy—has received a painting as a gift. But it's apparently sustained some damage. They're looking for someone to restore the painting, and I thought of you. What do you say to that?"

"I don't know. I'd have to see the painting first to know if I could do what they're asking for."

"I see what you mean. Look, why don't I ask them to send the painting to me? You can come over and look at it and see what you think. What do you have to lose?"

# # #

Late afternoon sunlight filtered through a crack in the drapes that Father Joseph had pulled shut. Alone in his office, he carefully swaddled the painting in bubble paper before wrapping it in dark green cloth; there was no need to trouble the residents with the picture's blasphemous image. The woman at *Servientes Mundi* had put him in touch with the artist's agent, and he explained to Raymond Chartrier what needed to be done: removing the image of the satyr.

"I can't make any promises, Father, but we'll do our best to help you." It didn't sound overly encouraging, but for the moment, it was the best Father Joseph could come up with.

The painting was delivered a week later. Raymond found it propped up against the receptionist's desk and carried it into his office. Curious to see the offending image, he hastened to remove the wrapping. His eye was drawn to the evil satyr, but once Raymond was able to look beyond it to the rest of the painting, he thought that the request made sense. But would Li be up to the task? Raymond hung the wrapping over the painting—he didn't want to get involved in explanations should anyone come into his office—and spent the morning doing his day job.

# # #

They had agreed to meet on Li's day off. Unknown to Raymond, Li had considered calling Raymond and telling him he was ill; ever since the encounter with Bruno he felt apprehensive each time he left his apartment. But, afraid of disappointing Raymond, he showed up at his office, albeit twenty minutes late. Raymond was relieved when the receptionist announced that he had a visitor; he had begun to worry that Li had had second thoughts. The painter looked so small and forlorn, so out of place in the open plan space filled with young engineers glued to their computers, that Raymond invited Li to lunch before showing him the painting; perhaps a bellyful of food would put him in a positive mood.

Over lunch, Raymond did his best to draw Li into conversation, but the painter seemed so…apprehensive. Was he worried that he would not be able to do the job? Raymond began to regret having gotten involved; this meal was certainly not enhancing his life experience. As the waiter cleared away their plates—at least Li had polished off the *endives au jambon*—Raymond asked if he wanted dessert, but Li shook his head. Raymond would have liked a *crème brulée,* but he settled for just an espresso before they returned to the office.

Li stood next to Raymond's desk as the engineer lifted the wrapping. An intake of breath: where is the toilet, please? His forehead was damp, and Raymond, afraid that Li was going to be sick, took him by the elbow and guided him into the hallway to the door marked *Toilettes.*

Several minutes passed. As Raymond wondered whether he should see if I needed help, the painter walked back into his office.

"Are you all right?"

"Yes, I think I have a stomach flu."

"Here, please sit down." Raymond hesitated, then continued, "As I told you, this painting was given to a home for retired clergy, and they were, of course, very shocked by the image of the satyr. Otherwise, it's a beautiful painting—don't you agree—and they asked the folks at *Servientes Mundi*, where you're on exhibit, if they knew someone who could remove the figure. So, what do you think? Could you fix the painting so it only depicts the joyous scene?"

Li sat, bent slightly forward, his hands resting on his knees, staring at the painting. Voices from the open-plan space drifted in through the cracks around the door; otherwise, the office was silent. Raymond held his breath, waiting for the painter to speak. At last, he did. "Yes," he said, "I can remove that ugly image. In fact, I can make the painting more beautiful. Can you drive me back to my home?"

"I'm afraid I have work to do here, but we have a car service I can call. Just let me know if you need to buy anything, and I will pay for it."

Li smiled for the first time since he walked into Raymond's office. "No, I have everything I need; thanks anyway."

# # #

The first thing Li did when he returned home was to undo the wrapping and place the Infant Bacchus painting on his easel. He felt like a parent whose child had disappeared and was happily found. He'd never understood the workings of the universe, only that you had to accept what life handed out to you as best you could. And today, the universe had returned his painting to him. The infant Bacchus had been a work in progress when Bruno reappeared and forced him to desecrate the tableau. But now, the universe had given him the opportunity to complete the work. He made himself a pot of tea and looked forward to getting started tomorrow.

# # #

The satyr had disappeared, covered by a pale wash. Li contemplated replacing the evil image with the figure he had outlined initially. But the painting's owner had requested that the image be removed, and he worried that if he painted in another version of the satyr, his work would be destroyed. So, instead, he added the tree that had been replaced by the satyr. Lastly, he applied the finishing touches that Bruno's appearance had interrupted. To the untrained eye, his tableau could have passed for a painting by Nicolas Poussin or, at least, one done in his style. Now all that remained was to call

Raymond Chartrier to tell him the job was completed. After putting all his love and attention into creating his own version of the Infancy of Bacchus, Li, like an owner losing a beloved pet, was overcome with chagrin at the thought of losing it once again.

Li, his voice flat and devoid of emotion, called Raymond, "Your painting, I've fixed it."

"Really? So soon? That's great."

"I guess so." Li was not given to cheery outbursts, but still, his lack of energy troubled Raymond. As Li's manager, he felt he had to do something to lift Li's spirits. "Listen, why don't we drive down and deliver the painting in person to the priests? I'm sure they would be delighted to meet the man who saved their painting."

A long moment of silence, and then "Yes, why not?"

"All right then, I'll make the arrangements and let you know." Afterward Raymond reflected that Li had not uttered more than a dozen words. Could you call that a conversation?

CHAPTER SIXTY-THREE

Toulouse

IT WAS TIME TO TAKE down the exhibition at *Servientes Mundi.* Since he and Li were going to Toulouse, Raymond Chartrier brought the painting of the frolicking infants with him; as he'd told Li, they would deliver it to the priests in person. But when they arrived at the exhibition, Raymond couldn't resist showing the painting to the woman who'd contacted him in the first place. "So, this is the famous painting," she gushed. "I wonder if Father Joseph would lend it to us now that the exhibition is over."

"I don't know, but if you like, I can ask him."

# # #

Li had made it a habit of studying faces to discover the person beneath the flesh. Jacques Mornnais—evil and calculating; Bruno—cruel, with a dark soul; Raymond Chartrier—kind and well-meaning. And as he listened to the priest sitting at his desk. "Thank you so much for transforming an abomination into something of beauty." He took in the lined forehead and the skin sagging around the man's neck; the eyes—alert but judgmental; and the mouth—thin lips that could be friendly but also stern.

"It is I who thank you," replied Li, "for giving me the opportunity."

Raymond Chartrier, who until now had been silent, spoke: "Father, I told the people at *Serientes Mundi* what Li here had done; now that the exhibition has finished, the walls are again bare, and they were wondering if you might be willing to lend them the painting—just for a short time—so that their visitors might have the chance to admire it." The way Raymond uttered this phrase, the words coming fast one after the other, made it seem that he had rehearsed his pitch.

Li kept his gaze on Father Joseph and saw his eyes weighing the pros and cons of giving up the painting he'd just received. The old priest was about to speak when one of the novices knocked on the door and entered the room.

"Excuse me," he said as he approached Father Joseph, "but it's important." Although he bent over to speak to the old priest, his words carried across the desk: "The hospice called; it's about Father Paul; they need to speak to you."

As the novice relayed the message, this time in a more subdued voice, Li watched as Father Jospeh's lips twisted from one expression to the next: annoyance, then disdain, while his eyes took on a worried look. The priest rose and walked around his desk.

"You'll have to excuse me. There's something I need to attend to." Then he seemed to remember Raymond's request, "Yes," he said, "let them keep the painting for now." After Father Joseph left the room, the two men wrapped the tableau and drove to Toulouse, where they presented it to the administrators at *Servientes Mundi.*

CHAPTER SIXTY-FOUR

Toulouse

BRUNO'S PLANS FOR FATHER PAUL having been momentarily thwarted, his mind returned to his other obsessions: Jacques and the painters. His lip curled as he thought about how he'd forced Li to deface his painting. Li: Bruno's mind jumped to the nightmarish view of the Château d'Hélène that he'd seen outside the building on Rue Nineau, and he suddenly felt the urge to go over there and have another look. An idea took hold: he'd buy the painting and show it to Jacques when he caught up with him.

But when he arrived at the stately building, the courtyard was bare. *What the fuck,* he muttered as he strode past two cars parked in the empty space where the painting had stood. Inside, he saw that Li's paintings no longer adorned the walls: *merde,* the exhibition was over. Where were the paintings now? He remembered seeing Li with a man he guessed was his agent; how could he get in touch with him? Then he recognized the woman he'd seen before—the one with the big tits—intending to ask her about purchasing the painting that had stood in the courtyard. But he stopped, frozen in place, when he saw the painting of the infant Bacchus *sans* the satyr. *That's not possible; how could this be?* Bruno approached the painting and stood so close that it looked like his nose was touching the canvas. But there was no sign of the evil satyr, just a tree.

"Excuse me, sir." It was the bitch behind the desk; had she recognized him? He heard her say, "Please step back from the painting, sir."

I'd like to slap that voice down her throat; instead, Bruno forced himself to be pleasant. "I was just admiring that painting; it's of the infant Bacchus, right? And it reminds me of other paintings by Nicolas Poussin. You wouldn't know if that's a genuine Poussin?"

Relieved by his gentle tone and the fact that he was not staring at her breasts, she offered the information destined to ruin Bruno's day: "No, I wouldn't know anything about that. The painting belongs to the clergy; it had been damaged, and Ma Zhen's agent helped them get it fixed. And soon, we'll return it to them."

Thoughts of the painting of Château d'Hélène faded away, his quest for Father Paul coming back to center stage: "The clergy? Who might that be?"

"Oh, just an old-age home for priests, I think." When the man stood silently, giving no sign of moving away, the woman lowered her eyes and busied herself shuffling papers, indicating that she had nothing further to say.

# # #

Bruno sat in a café on *Place Saint-Stéphane*, reliving the morning's events. *Fucking Li.* So, the priests at the *Résidence* had gotten him to rework the infant Bacchus painting. His first impulse was to punish Li until he realized that his plan had worked; the fact that the priests had asked Li to remove the satyr meant that they'd seen the painting and were shocked by the scene. No, perhaps he ought to thank Li for a job well done and, while he was at it, ask about buying the depiction of Château d'Hélène that had stood outside *Servientes Mundi.*

CHAPTER SIXTY-FIVE

Vitry-sur-Seine

BRUNO PARKED A FEW DOORS from Li's apartment, sat in the car, and waited for him to return home from work. A gust of wind blew an assortment of cans and plastic shopping bags along the sidewalk, reminding him of Marseille. Visions of Sauveur and Jacques arose, pulling his mind back to Château d'Hélène, the reason for today's visit. In the distance, Li emerged from the late afternoon gloom like a slow-moving shadow, hands in his pockets, shoulders hunched up to his ears.

Li unlocked the door; the apartment was cold—it smelled of despair and turpentine. He plugged in the radiator but kept his jacket on as he reheated a pot of soup he'd made the night before. A knock on the door as the liquid started to bubble; *it must be one of my neighbors,* he thought and cracked open the door to see what they wanted. *It's probably someone coming around asking to borrow money*; it wouldn't be the first time. But it was Bruno who pushed his way in, throwing Li off-balance and onto the floor.

Li picked himself up; "What do you want now? If you've come to kill me, then just get it over with." He realized his soup was boiling and went to the stove to turn off the flame. *Should I try to throw the soup at him? What's the point? He'll manage to kill me anyway."* He sat down on a chair and waited.

"I'm not going to kill you, Li"—Bruno seemed to be saying that a lot lately. "Our score is settled. I've come to see you to buy your painting of the château that stood outside the exhibition. Where can I find it? "

"You want to *buy* the painting, not cut it into shreds or ask me to add some gruesome image?"

"Oh no, believe me, I want to keep it just as it is."

What choice do I have anyway? Li looked in his phone to find Raymond Chartrier's cell phone number, fished around on the table for a scrap of paper, and wrote it down along with Raymond's name. "This is my agent. You can call him if you really want to buy the painting."

Bruno slipped the paper into his pocket, pulled up the only other chair, and seated himself across from Li, leaning forward, his hands on his knees. "And there's something else," he said.

Li stiffened: *Okay, here it comes.*

"Yeah, I wanted to thank you. For adding the satyr, it did the job."

What job? What is he talking about?

"You look puzzled, so let me explain. There was a priest who assaulted me many times when I was a young boy. He made me who I am today. And your painting was part of my revenge, to frighten him. And it worked."

"What do you mean, 'assaulted' you?"

"What do you think? Father Paul used me—and other boys—to satisfy his sexual desires."

"What did you say his name was?"

"Father Paul, why do you ask?"

The room was silent, but for the whirring of the refrigerator. Li shivered, not so much from the foul-smelling cold as from understanding Btuno's cruelty for the first time. A long hesitation, and then he spoke: "My agent was contacted by the people where my exhibition took place. They asked if he knew someone who could remove the image and restore the painting, and Raymond wound up asking me to do it. When I had completed my work, we drove down to Gaillac to return it to the priests. And while we were there, a young man came in and told the priest-in-residence that the hospice had called about someone called Father Paul. That could be the same person."

Li watched Bruno—saw his cheeks turn pink, his eyes glittering—and he waited for the big man to speak. An eternity passed, or so it seemed to Li, until Bruno rose, shook his hand, and patted him on the back. "Thanks, and *adieu*," he said, walking out the door.

This time, Li dared to hope that he'd seen the last of Bruno.

CHAPTER SIXTY-SIX

Toulouse

BRUNO SEARCHED THE INTERNET FOR 'Hospices in Toulouse.' Over the following weeks, he visited the hospitals and old age homes on his list: *I'm trying to find my uncle. I've lost track of him, but one of my cousins told me he's in poor health and in a hospice in Toulouse, but they didn't know the name. His name is Father Paul, and I wondered if he might be one of your patients. I'd like to see him before it's too late.*

On some days, he sounded convincing enough for the receptionist to look through the database; at other times, he got nothing more than a skeptical look. *I'm sorry, but we don't give out that information.*

He sat on his bed and looked at the dog-eared list he'd copied. Only two places remained. *Should I even bother? What the fuck, what do I have to lose?*

It was a small, square building painted light brown; the color reminded him of chocolate milk. Inside, clutching his motorcycle helmet to his chest like a talisman, he approached the young woman seated at the reception desk. "It's *my uncle; we're trying to find him,"* he began. He managed to sound as if he was pleading, his eyes blinking rapidly, then his head cast downward. Perhaps the young woman felt sorry for him; perhaps she didn't know any better. She pressed a few keys on her computer: "I'm sorry, but there's no one by that name here." Bruno, discouraged, sighed, this time his emotions real, not feigned: "I've looked all over for him, I don't know what to do." The young woman thought for a moment. "I'm from Gaillac, and there's a hospice outside the town; Saint-Michel's. Why don't you ask there?"

Bruno's fingers turned white as he gripped his helmet. He swallowed, took a deep breath, and tried to find his voice. "Thank you, that's a good idea. I'll give it a try." He forced himself to walk outside slowly, then sat on his bike and waited for his heart to stop thumping before heading back to Rue des Arts. As he drove, a vision of the priest's face was superimposed on the highway, the wheels of his motorcycle smashing it again and again.

# # #

Father Paul wasn't doing well, said the hospice director. She hesitated, then asked whether Father Joseph thought it best to administer the last rites. "Is it really that serious," he asked. He'd sent Father Paul to the hospice not so much for medical care as to put some distance between him (and, by implication, the *Résidence*) and his stalker. As she heard his question, the director started to have second thoughts.

"Well, I don't know, really. He complains that he's having trouble breathing, but aside from his being asthmatic, we haven't found anything else. It's more of a precaution, I guess."

"Let's wait a bit and see how things develop. You'll keep me informed, won't you?"

# # #

Father Paul sat in bed, his head propped against a pillow. His room overlooked the Tarn, and he gazed across the river at the façade of the Abbey on the opposite bank. The trees blocked his view of the square in front of the Abbey, but in his imagination, he saw the faded brick exterior of the *Résidence.* He smiled inwardly, feeling the warm comfort of the safety provided by the hospice. There was no way Bruno Edremal could find him here. The sharp pains in his belly had disappeared, yet he knew better than to let on how much better he was feeling; otherwise, he'd risk being sent back to the *Résidence.* He'd started to complain that he was having trouble breathing; that ought to be enough to keep him here.

Most of his books and papers had remained at the *Résidence,* part of the fiction that his stay in the hospice was only temporary. The novices had packed up his clothing—now hanging in the closet—and personal items. As well, they'd brought over his black canvas bag, slouching in the corner opposite his bed. Father Paul's eye fell on the bag; he longed to open it and access the pleasure hidden there but dared not to. There was no lock on the door; anyone could come barging in at any time for whatever reason. So, he had to content himself with focusing on the bag and the secrets it held for him.

CHAPTER SIXTY-SEVEN

Gaillac

AN INTERNET SEARCH FOR HOSPICE Saint-Michel came up empty, and Bruno started to have second thoughts. What if the girl was mistaken? What if she'd just made up a story to get rid of him? The only way to find out if the hospice existed was to go to Gaillac.

An old woman was dragging an overloaded shopping cart behind her when Bruno pulled up. He began to ask directions to the hospice, but taking one look at his face, she hurried away, cart and all. *Fuck.* He saw a newspaper kiosk on the corner; perhaps he'd have better luck there. And he did. "The hospice, yeah, it's over there," the man pointed his finger to a spot behind Bruno's head.

"Where, over there?"

"Sorry, on the other side of the river, facing the Abbey. It's up on a hill; you can't miss it."

"Thanks."

# # #

Bruno drove to the Abbey and parked his bike. He walked down to the riverbank and sat on a bench, gazing at the building on the hill overlooking the river. It was a long, low structure, only two stories high. He didn't know it, but the building had been a hunting lodge for a family of local aristocrats. When the male line died out, the remaining direct descendants offered the building to the brothers of the Saint-Michel abbey, who turned it into a hospice.

When Bruno was in Lyon, he'd gone to Father Paul's room, and then he ran out, suddenly uncertain about what to do. When he'd returned, Father Paul was gone. But this time, any uncertainty was gone. Bruno knew what he had to do, and he was confident that the *how* would come to him at the right moment.

Bruno walked back to where he'd parked his bike. He drove to the outskirts of the town, pulling up to a McDonald's in an industrial park. The golden arches were wedged between two office complexes; Bruno's smirk returned when he saw 'Wind Power Unlimited' among the names of the resident companies. Wasn't that one of the companies mentioned in the papers lying around the apartment of his unfortunate neighbor? He'd taken care of that guy, just as he'd take care of the priest; it was a good omen for the night ahead.

The McDo was closing. He took his food and sat on his bike in the mostly deserted parking lot. No need to rush; he ate his meal slowly as there was nothing to do until night fell. Afterward, he rode back to the Abbey, parked his bike, and sat in the same spot, watching as the lights in the hospice were extinguished one by one.

The night was clear; pinholes of light glowed in the black sky, and Bruno felt they were sending their energy to him. When the hospice remained dark—there were occasional pricks of light, but they were too weak for him to see—he returned to his bike, rode across the bridge, and parked in the woods behind the building.

It was time to take his revenge.

CHAPTER SIXTY-EIGHT

BRUNO, DRESSED IN BLACK, STOOD at the edge of the woods; no more than a shadow, he surveyed the rear of the hospice. He wore a small backpack; it was black too. No sign of surveillance cameras, only darkness in the few windows on that side of the building. He saw a rear entrance; he'd break in that way—he felt it wiser than trying the front door.

He examined the lock and fiddled around in his backpack until he found the correct ring of keys and started to see which one fit. It took a few minutes, but then the key turned in the lock, and he was inside, looking down a long, unlit corridor.

Next, he pulled on a headlamp and turned it on. He explored a hallway leading off the corridor and discovered it led to the kitchen. Retracing his steps and continuing down the corridor, he found himself at the entry. On one side, there was a small office; he looked for a computer, but there was none. The smirk returned, "*Lucky for me, this place probably hasn't changed in a hundred years.*" His luck continued; on the desk was an open ledger listing the entries and departures of the hospice's residents. On the top page, he saw Father Paul's name, and next to it, he saw his room number: 6.

He started to leave the office when he heard footsteps; it sounded like they were coming from the floor above. Nevertheless, he crouched behind the desk, waiting. Then he heard a toilet flushing, footsteps, and a door closing. Of course, old people with weak bladders. And perhaps there was a night nurse as well? He'd have to be on the lookout.

Bruno crept up the stairway—it was covered by a worn carpet, threadbare in spots—that led to the first floor. Suddenly, as he reached the top of the stairway, a buzzer squawked like an angry bird, and he saw a thin beam of light in the hallway. He slid back down the stairs, hiding in the alcove beneath the stairway. A man's voice—for the holder of the beam of light was a man—was muttering loud enough for him to hear: *Merde, j'arrive, vieux con.* Well, that answered his question: there *was* a night nurse, and unfortunately, he'd have to deal with him. Bruno was at last positioned to take his revenge, and nothing was going to stop him.

# # #

The slow march of time: a door opened and closed, then opened and closed again. The night nurse's steady footsteps as he returned to his cubbyhole. It was fucking two o'clock in the morning, and he'd come straight from his day job; he was fucking tired and let the fucking *vieux cons* shove the buzzer up their asses. It was time to take a break. He put in his earbuds, stretched out on the floor, and fell asleep.

# # #

Silence rolled down the hallway and descended to the ground floor; Bruno, imagining the hospice walls rising and falling with each breath. He once again crept up the stairway, and when he reached the top, he stopped to listen. The snoring disturbed the emptiness; gingerly, he tiptoed toward an open door and saw the noise was coming from the night nurse. *That's a good boy; get some rest.*

Padding down the hallway, he stopped in front of the door with the number six painted on it. He felt a tingling in his fingers, and then a wave of energy moved up his arms, across his chest, and down his legs to his toes. It seemed to him that his whole life had been building up to this moment. Gently turning the doorknob, he stepped inside the room.

# # #

Bruno turned off his headlamp. Letting his eyes adjust to the obscurity—to the dark gray film hovering above the bed—he glimpsed the form of a body and heard the wheeze of air from an open mouth. Stepping closer, he recognized the beaklike nose, the pockmarked cheeks; yes, it was Father Paul. *We need some privacy;* he disconnected the alarm buzzer hanging from the bar on the side of the bed. Then he leaned over the priest, whispering in his ear the words that had been ready for so long: "It's time to wake up, Father; your time has come." The voice was low, the words, hard as rocks, crashed through the wall of sleep. Father Paul, disoriented (was he awake or dreaming?) opened his eyes and stared into the face of Bruno Edremal. A spasm ripped through his belly, and he had difficulty catching his breath. "What do you want," he gasped, the words getting caught in his throat.

"Having trouble speaking, are we? Perhaps you'd like a glass of water?" Bruno filled a plastic goblet and poured the liquid into Father Paul's mouth. "Here, have a drink." Father Paul coughed as the water rushed down his throat, spilling over his chin and onto his pajamas. "Is there a problem, Father?"

Another spasm rippled through Father Paul, his mouth puckering like a fish out of water.

"Are you afraid of drowning, Father?" The priest reached for the buzzer, pressed it, and pressed it again.

"No one is coming, Father. It's just the two of us like it was so many times in the past. And no one came to help me either. How does that feel? Well," he continued, "I will tell you how you made me feel."

Father Paul, his breathing labored, moved his hands to cover his ears. "No, no, that won't do, Father." When Bruno was a small child, the priest had seemed to him to be so big and powerful. And now, he was just a bag of bones. Bruno bent over the shrunken body, placed Father Paul's arms by his sides, and tucked the blanket securely under the mattress. "That's better. Now, you're going to listen to me."

The old priest's lips trembled. He tried to speak but he seemed to choke on his breath. Bruno pulled his chair close to Father Paul, and in a low voice, he started to talk to him. He recounted how Father Paul had abused him, how he had hurt him, and how dirty he felt afterward. The rough stubble on his cheeks. The curly black chest hairs. He couldn't tell his mother; he knew she would not believe him even if he did. The horror of the retreats and the camping trips. He said that he knew about the other boys the priest had mistreated and how their lives, like his, had been ruined.

As Bruno spoke, Father Paul stared at the ceiling, his unblinking eyes wide with fear. A coughing fit racked his body, the waves of pain in his midsection unremitting; for a time, his shallow breathing returned, and then he was still.

Bruno now was still as well. For the first time since his childhood, he was crying. Crying for his lost life, for the lost lives of his friends. He looked at the inert body. The trauma of almost drowning had awakened his memories, and he felt that the cycle was coming to an end. But not quite yet.

Bruno stood up, walked to the closet, and pushed the few wire hangers. He was looking for some clue to the old priest's perversions. *There's nothing here*, he thought, until he noticed an old black wheelie bag in the corner. With his knife, he sliced through the fabric and started to remove the contents. At first, there was nothing of interest, just some old religious stuff. Then, an intake of breath as he pulled out Father Paul's favorite magazine. *A pervert to his dying day. He's not going to take this secret to his grave.*

Bruno loosened the blanket, placed Father Paul's hands on his chest, and slipped the magazine under his fingers. He returned the rest of the contents to the wheelie bag. All that remained was to plug in the buzzer and leave.

# # #

The night nurse awoke with a start. Outside, the sky had turned pale gray. How long had he been asleep? *Merde.* It was quiet—no buzzers were ringing—but he had a feeling that something was off. He walked down the hallway, entering each of the residents' rooms to make sure they were breathing. *All good,* he breathed a sigh of relief until he opened the door to room number six. *He's too quiet,* he thought as he approached the bed. His stomach clenched: the old man's eyes were open, and it was obvious that he was dead. Then he noticed the magazine in the old priest's hands, and although the Director would later swear him to secrecy, it was soon known that Father Paul had died while viewing child pornography.

CHAPTER SIXTY-NINE

Mélandère

HE FELT LIGHTER, THE SHAME and sadness were gone. It seemed that he could not get enough sleep; he would sleep for twelve or fourteen hours, go for a long walk, and return to his bed. His dreams of Father Paul had disappeared, as the fog burns away in the sunshine.

Jacques Mornnais moved to the forefront of his mind. He told himself that once he found Jacques, he'd be free to live his life unencumbered by thought. At that moment, it didn't occur to him that he would always be encumbered by one desire for vengeance or another, that his issue with Jacques was not the source of his thoughts, but the consequence.

Jacques could be anyplace, and yet Bruno was convinced that when he found the place, in hindsight, it would seem logical. Where to start; could Jacques be hiding out in Mélandère? Bruno had been to the house at Roquebrune-sur-Argens only a few times. It was one of those places that had a certain charm when seen from the outside, but it was really a bit of a dump. Jacques had put in a modern *en suite* bathroom for his use. When they all stayed at Mélandère, Bruno and Tarek had had to cope with the old bathroom with its cracked porcelain, and the tepid water that came in a thin stream from the showerhead.

He didn't care for Mélandère, but it might make sense to start his search there. He left Toulouse at midday, and by early evening he had pulled into the courtyard at the back of the stately Italianate summer villa. The garbage bin was empty, dead leaves were scattered where the wind had blown them. The tall grass on the front lawn had turned yellow in the summer heat.

Confident that no one had been to the house recently, he pried open one of the shutters on the ground-floor, broke a window and let himself into the house. The air inside was hot and musty. The moldings and the furniture were covered in a layer of yellow dust, blown in by the mistral.

He went into the kitchen; opened the rear door and went outside to remove a small bag of food from his saddlebags. It wasn't a lot, but he didn't intend to stay for very long. Suddenly he heard the whir of the refrigerator. *What the fuck, the electricity is still on.*

Bruno searched the house, room by room, for some clue as to Jacques' whereabouts. There was an unmade bed in the master bedroom, but when had Jacques been there? In fact, Jacques and Mila had last been at Mélandère in April 2010, when Mila had been killed by a car bomb as they were preparing to leave. It was Eugene Spector who had told him that Mila was dead, but as for when Jacques had been at Mélandère, Bruno knew nothing; at the time, he was in Lyon trying to remember who he was.

When he had finished his tour of the house, he went outside to get his toiletries. It was then that he saw the steel door to the cellar vault. *Of course, I'd forgotten that Jacques stored artwork here.* His hand went instinctively to the number pad, and he keyed in a code. The door swung open, and he was greeted by a whiff of cold, filtered air. He had expected to see the paintings lined up against the wall, but the room was empty aside from a pile of bubble paper in one corner. Another thought arose: *the fucker, he's moved the paintings to Montenegro.*

Back inside the house, he opened a bottle of Badoit and took a few gulps. The water was warm, but the bubbles soothed his throat. Carrying his bottle of water, he walked through the reception area. There were frescos in one of the rooms. He remembered Jacques saying that the former owners of the house had instructed the painters to put portraits of the family members in the murals. *Where are they now? Probably long dead and buried.* He felt an urge to destroy those faces, remove the last trace of their existence, but the thought was pushed aside by another: *could Jacques be in Montenegro?*

Bruno flopped down on a sofa in one of the reception rooms. The cushions were no longer plump, the velvet upholstery was faded, but it felt good to stretch his legs after the long ride. He stared at the ceiling where the paint had started to peel, leaving a web of fine lines.

He tried to remember Montenegro. They had gone there once, years ago. Jacques' house was a sprawling white structure, like another fucking château. It stood on a hill, overlooking the small village below. Jacques had bought up the village: "Welcome to my fiefdom," he had said with a sneer.

But where was his fucking house? A car had picked them up on their arrival; he'd had a few drinks during the flight, and he'd fallen asleep on the drive from the airport. He didn't think he'd ever known the name of the village, yet he felt that some clue to its location was hidden in his memory.

Eugene, the American. He had helped Bruno when he'd arrived in Lyon, his memory wiped away when he'd almost drowned. Eugene had been looking for Jacques, and they'd arrived at Château d'Hélène at the same time. The front door had been open, but Jacques was not there. In searching the house, Eugene had come across boxes full of Jacques' files, that he'd taken away. And Bruno had found a pile of cash. But his quest was incomplete; he needed to find Jacques, and he felt the same was true for the American. Hadn't he asked about Jacques when they met at the red-haired cow's restaurant? So, he still looking for Jacques Mornnais as well.

Toulouse. Bruno had seen Eugene there; he was with the blonde, wasn't her name Alex? When Bruno returned to Toulouse tomorrow, he'd look for him. He checked his cell phone. And smiled. He still had the American's phone number; it might be just as easy to call him.

Bruno drove into Roquebrune-sur-Argens as the sun was setting. He walked the town's mostly empty streets, hoping that the stroll would clear his mind, and allow him to dredge up some past memory from Montenegro. But all he experienced was a gnawing hunger. He had an early dinner before returning to Mélandère, where he went to sleep in the unmade bed. Before he left early the next morning, he closed the shutter that he'd pried open.

But he left the shards of glass where they had fallen, nor did he bother to remove the half-empty bottle of Badoit that he'd left on an end table in the reception room.

CHAPTER SEVENTY

Trubenne

WHILE EUGENE WAS IN PARIS, Alex was on her hands and knees, cleaning the octagonal terracotta floor tiles; after the visitors had toured the vineyard, they would come to this room for a wine tasting. The *tomettes,* as they were called, were in various shades of pale reddish brown. They brought to mind the color of dried blood, but no blood had been shed at Château de Trubenne, if you didn't çount the man who'd been eaten by the *sangliers.*

The floor had been laid down when the château was built, over three hundred years ago. François Tran had found replacements for the tiles that were cracked or broken, and Alex could already imagine visitors lifting a glass of wine when the room was restored to its former glory.

Thoughts of Alex's cousin Charlotte, who had been killed along with her lover Sauveur Paoli, mingled with daydreams of the success of the vineyard. She recalled the day that Sauveur had taken them sailing, remembered the sounds of gunfire while she took photos of the *Calanques*, the majestic limestone cliffs. Charlotte had been killed along with Sauveur, and Alex had been wounded in the attack. Although she had recovered, a heavy sadness remained beneath her calm, smiling exterior. But today, as she scrubbed the *tomettes,* the sadness morphed into anger. Why had the shooting occurred?

She had heard the phrase "wrong place, wrong time," when she lay in her hospital bed, but that was of little help in understanding why.

She felt a drop of perspiration roll down the bridge of her nose, landing on the tile she was scrubbing. The drop was a perfect oval, the shape of an egg. It reminded her of another egg shape: the suntanned shaven head of Charles Paoli, Sauveur's cousin. She had meant to call him when they returned from their trip to Paris last June, but it had slipped her mind.

What was it that he had said? "*I do not want to disturb you, Madame Thornhill, but if I can ever be of help, please do not hesitate to call on me*." He had handed her his card, held her hand for a moment in his two hands, bowed his head and walked away. Charles Paoli. *Let's see if he can be of help.*

# # #

After Charlotte's funeral, Alex had closed up the house in Vauban. She had given most of Charlotte's clothing away, but she kept a purple collapsible umbrella and a black cloche hat. She didn't use either article, but they reminded her of Charlotte, and she kept them in one of her dresser drawers.

In her haste to leave the house, Alex had scooped up every piece of paper, every flyer for pizza home delivery, every coupon from the supermarket, and thrown them into a small tote bag that she'd tossed into the back of her bedroom closet. She fished around through the contents of the bag that were now strewn on her bed and found the card that Charles Paoli had given to her. It was a cheap card, the kind that cost five Euros for one hundred. When it came to information, Charles Paoli was clearly a minimalist: the card gave only his name and his cell phone number. His message was clear: I don't need a piece of cardboard with embossed type to impress people.

What would Charlotte do? She'd call the man, that's what she'd do. With no further thought, Alex called Charles Paoli. The phone rang and then switched to voicemail.

"Mr. Paoli, this is Alexia Thornhill. You came to see me in Marseille and said to call if you could help. I'd be grateful if you could call me back. Thank you."

Alex went back to scrubbing the floor and didn't hear her phone ring. Later, after she had showered and dressed, she found a message from Charles Paoli; he gave her another number and asked her to call him back. *Who was Charles Paoli, anyway? No second thoughts. Just call him.* This time Charles Paoli answered the phone. He was pleasant if not a bit overly formal: "I'm glad to hear from you, my dear lady. How can I help you?"

Alex took a deep breath: "It's about the accident; I guess I'm trying to understand why we were attacked. No one has told us anything except to say that Charlotte and I were collateral damage. But why was your cousin killed? And by whom?"

"I thought you would have heard by now," he said.

"Heard what?"

"My cousin bought a painting from a man named Jacques Mornnais. And when he discovered that the tableau was a forgery, we believe that he called Mornnais and asked for his money back. And rather than pay up, Mornnais arranged for Sauveur to be removed permanently."

Alex felt her throat tightening; for a moment she stopped breathing altogether. Her voice came out in a squeak: "In that case, why haven't the police arrested this Mornnais?"

"There isn't any formal proof, and as you know, the shooting was done by three thugs." He hesitated before continuing: "It may be of some comfort to you to know that the killers were found and properly punished."

"I didn't know that. The police have said nothing to us."

"The police were not involved."

Charles Paoli spoke slowly. His voice was deep and calm, he could have been telling her about a book he had read, rather than the settling of scores. Alex was frightened, but she felt that there was still more to learn from him.

"I see. Properly punished. Okay. But what about Jacques Mornnais, I mean, isn't he the one who ordered the killing?"

"What about him?"

"I mean, where is he, why haven't the police arrested him?"

"Dear lady, believe me, I would like to help you, but I do not know Mr. Mornnais' whereabouts"

"He's alive then, you're sure of that?"

Charles Paoli sighed, "Yes, to the best of my knowledge, he's alive, but he's not in France. I'm afraid that is all that I know."

Alex suspected that Charles Paoli knew more, but she was sure that she'd gotten all that she could out of him. *He means that's all he's going to tell me*. At least she had the confirmation that Jacques Mornnais was alive. Eugene would be relieved to learn that.

# # #

La Ciotat

Charles Paoli poured a measure of *pastis*; the golden liquid turned a milky white as he added ice cubes and then water to his glass. He lit a cigar and adjusted his ample form on a chaise longue at the poolside. His gaze fell upon the bay below, the water thick with blueness. He should have felt at peace in the late afternoon, but neither the drink, nor the cigar, nor the splendid view could erase the memory of Sauveur's death.

He understood that Alexia Thornhill wanted to find the man who was responsible for her cousin's murder, and he was sincere when he had told her that he wanted to help her. But the best he could do was to let her know that Jacques Mornnais was alive. He could not tell her that the despicable man was in Montenegro. For the time being Jacques Mornnais was protected by *raison d'état,* and even he, Charles Paoli, was powerless to act as he wished.

All he needed to do was to be patient and bide his time. Eventually, the government would find a replacement for Jacques, and then they would abandon him—he was sure of that. And when they did, he would go to Montenegro and do what was necessary.

He felt sorry for Alexia Thornhill, but he could not let her win the race to find Jacques Mornnais. She didn't know he was in Montenegro, and it would have to stay that way.

CHAPTER SEVENTY-ONE

Trubenne

ALEX DROVE TO NÎMES TO meet Eugene's train.

"How did it go in Paris?"

"As expected. I explained that we were prepared for a court battle, and I'm pretty sure I convinced him that he'd be wasting his time."

"Why wasn't he convinced when I said the same thing?"

"I already told you. He's one of those men who doesn't take women seriously. He's an asshole, what else can I say?"

Alex didn't entirely believe Eugene. What else had he said to Vital? She decided that she didn't need to know.

He studied her profile as she concentrated on the road, the aquiline nose, the firm chin.

"What are you thinking? I've got the feeling that there's something on your mind," he said.

"There is, actually. Did I ever tell you that a cousin of Sauveur's—a man named Charles Paoli—came to see me when I was still at Charlotte's house in Marseille? He walked up to me as I was putting my key in the lock, gave me his card, and said to call him if I needed help."

"No Alex, you never mentioned that to me."

"I guess that I quickly forgot about it, and then, while I was scrubbing the floor, I remembered. And I called him to ask about the accident."

"And…"

"He told me two things. First, that the men who shot at us had been punished, but not by the police. He said it so matter-of-factly that I was afraid to ask him anything more. And second, that Jacques Mornnais is alive and living outside of France. He said he didn't know anything more. I think he knows where Jacques is, but he does not want to tell me, or perhaps he cannot."

"Interesting," he said. "When I was in Paris, I met a colleague who told me the same thing. Not that those thugs had been '*punished*' — I can imagine what that means — but that our friend Jacques was alive and protected by *raison d'état.* We could wait until they let him return, but I'll bet your friend Charles is eager to get his hands on Jacques as well. So, we need to figure out how to get to him first."

Alex continued to look straight ahead, but when they reached a roundabout, she turned to him: "And how are we going to do that?"

"I don't know. Perhaps something will turn up. For now, I'm looking forward to a cold beer and some quality time with you."

"Oh, in that order?"

"We'll see."

# # #

Toulouse

Two of the demons haunting Bruno had disappeared, leaving an empty space where his old terrors had resided. He felt on edge in his own skin, waiting for something to happen. And that something was finding Jacques Mornnais.

There was a large bookstore nearby. Bruno walked over to it and spent more than an hour browsing travel guides for southeast Europe. He thumbed through books on Montenegro, that little clump of land carved out of Serbia. He wasn't interested in the history of the place, just what it looked like. Bruno picked out four books full of color photos; if he studied them long enough, maybe a feeling of familiarity would jog his memory, and reveal where he'd been when he had visited there with Jacques.

On the way home, Bruno stopped at the barbershop for a haircut and to trim his beard. Back in his apartment, he showered for the second time that day. The icy stream of water seemed to shrink the empty spaces, at least for a while. He enjoyed the feeling, his body first tingling and then numb. Finally, he stepped out of the shower and wrapped a towel around his mid-section. Since he'd lost his memory, he hadn't paid much attention to his appearance; once, when he'd met Jacques for lunch, and the time he'd gone to *Servientes Mundi* and pretended to be a collector. Today, a good-looking man, if not for the emptiness in his eyes, stared back at him from the mirror above the sink. *Not too bad.* Gone were the bloodshot eyes and puffy cheeks from the time he worked for Jacques. The thought of Jacques pulled up another idea: the American, he needed to call him.

"It's me, Bruno," he said when Eugene answered.

"And how are you, my friend?"

"I think I know where Jacques is."

"Oh, yes?"

"Yeah. I had forgotten that he has a house in Montenegro."

A sliver of excitement ran through Eugene's voice, "That's great, Bruno. And where in Montenegro might that be?"

"I don't remember. But I'm working on it."

"Is there something I can do to help?"

"No, not really. But when I figure it out, I thought we could go to Montenegro together. We're still a team, right?"

"You bet."

"Okay, I'll call you."

Bruno looked at the pile of books on the table. It would be a lot of work to go through them. He'd probably have to read about the towns as well as look at the images. But if that were what it took to catch up with Jacques, he would do it.

It was time for dinner. The sun had not yet set as he walked over to Place Saint-Etienne. It was still warm, but the cool breeze meant that autumn was not far off. A young woman was seated at the table next to his. Her blonde hair was pulled back into a ponytail. She reminded him of Eugene's girlfriend Alex, but younger, less brittle.

He knew she had been looking at him, and when the waiter brought his bottle of Perrier, he poured some, lifted his glass, and smiled at her.

"It's a lovely evening, isn't it?"

Her cheeks turned rosy, "Yes, it is."

She spoke with an accent, and he guessed that she was a student; no doubt she'd just arrived in Toulouse for the academic year.

"Are you new to Toulouse? I can hear that you're not French."

"No, I'm English. I just arrived yesterday."

Bruno switched to English: "Then perhaps you'd let me show you around?"

The waiter returned to take his order. He considered offering to buy her dinner but thought better of it; that might scare her away. He told her about places to visit in Toulouse and then asked her if she had been to other cities in France. When she said yes, she'd spent a week in Paris, he talked about Paris. By the end of his meal, he had her phone number.

"Can I walk you back to your apartment," he asked. "You need to watch out for the drunks as the evening progresses." He chuckled inwardly as he heard himself utter those words. They walked down Rue Ninau, to reach her apartment near Le Grand Rond. Bruno's thoughts were focused on the girl, no longer on Father Paul. He could sense that she was debating whether to invite him up or not.

"I've got to get an early start tomorrow morning. Are you free for dinner tomorrow night?"

"Tomorrow?" She pretended to think whether she was free tomorrow: "Why yes, I guess I could be free."

"Great, I'll call you tomorrow then." He leaned over to exchange air kisses and headed back to his apartment and his books. *This is going to be easy.*

CHAPTER SEVENTY-TWO

October 2011
Paris

FOR VITAL VESLA DE TRUBENNE, Rue de Clignancourt in Paris's eighteenth *arrondissement* was another world, an alien planet from which he couldn't take off soon enough. Real estate agents, intent on selling the potential of an apartment at that location, referred to the neighborhood as "cosmopolitan," a shorthand way of saying that part of its population was of African or Middle Eastern origin. Vital made his way past small groups crowded around tables of *bonneteau*, the French version of three-card Monte, the players and shills ready to pick up and run the moment a police officer came into view.

He pursed his lips in distaste. This street, with its crowds and its smells, was light years from the sixteenth arrondissement. The margin calls had more than wiped out his financial cushion, they'd left him seriously in debt, and he had no choice but to sell his string of sex shops in the nation's capital. He had hoped to leverage his share of the vineyard at Trubenne to pay off his debts, but the visit of his cousin's boyfriend had put an end to that idea. *The fucking American. Where had he gotten those photos?*

Of course, it was not surprising that the purchaser was based here. After all, he could hardly expect to find him in the vicinity of his law offices in Paris' golden triangle. Still, it annoyed him that he had been forced to come here, rub shoulders with the Blacks and Arabs.

He walked into an insurance agent's storefront and was shown into a room at the rear. The room was clean, it smelled of fresh paint, and the office furniture looked new. "Hello, Mr. Vital, so nice of you to come here," said a heavyset, tan-colored man, his bald head shining in the fluorescent light.

They shook hands, and the negotiation began. Vital pointed out that the man had offered only half of what the shops were worth; he could hardly be expected to give them away.

"Yes, Mr. Vital (Vital hated being addressed by his first name in this way), but you need to see my problem. You're a lawyer, and as you know, you're not allowed to operate this kind of business, so for me, the shops are well, how should I put it, they're tainted by your illegality. Of course, you may find someone who looks at the situation differently, but if you don't, then…" The tan-colored man shrugged his shoulders; he may have had his office on Rue de Clignancourt, but he did not lack negotiation skills.

"The shops are not tainted, as you put it; it's just that I've chosen to divest at this time." It was a weak argument, and Vital knew it. He stood up to leave. The heavyset man laughed, "Okay, okay, Mr. Vital, don't be so upset." And he raised his price enough so that Vital knew he could not do better elsewhere.

A week later, the contract had been signed, and the funds arrived in an offshore account. Vital felt relieved that it was all over and that he'd managed to cover his losses. Yet, he wondered what had happened to Antoine Tipette. There was a last outstanding bill for services rendered. He'd intended to cancel the invoice if the merger went through, but now he'd not only lost money. The consultant had disappeared without paying.

Thinking that a good workout would clear his mind, he left the office early and went to his gym. An exercise class was scheduled to start in a few minutes. He was tempted to join but then reflected that while the class was predominantly female—a good thing—almost all of the women were in much better shape than he was. But bugger that—he'd take his place at the back of the room. A squat, muscular young man strode into the room, his bulging biceps adorned with elaborate tattoos. That was unfortunate; Vital preferred to watch the female instructors in their form-fitting garments.

He opted instead for a session on the treadmill. After a slow start, he increased the speed, and with each stride, he relived all the steps in the sale of his sex shops. His face was red with effort, but he kept at it, fueled by anger. *Fucking unfair, that's what it is, fucking unfair.* It was his last thought before he fell backwards on the treadmill.

The Vesla de Trubenne clan turned out for the funeral. Vital's wife Anne looked solemn, or perhaps bored, as he was laid to rest in the family plot. There would be the usual administrative hassles, the government eager to take its share of the estate. Luckily, her lover, a man she met on her morning run, was a lawyer as well, and he'd help her through the regulatory maze.

# # #

"Let's go get a drink," Eugene said to Alex and Richard when they returned from the cemetery.

"I'll take you to my club," said Richard.

"Great," said Alex. Eugene was curious but said nothing.

They were seated in a corner alcove, the pale October sunlight filtering through an opening in the heavy drapes. "What a wasted life," said Richard as he sipped his green tea. "Nothing to show for it but an obsession with money and a loveless, childless marriage."

Richard was pretty obsessed with making money, and he and Chloe had no children, although they did love each other. Alex remained silent.

"The idea of his wanting a share in Trubenne, how ridiculous," he continued. He turned to Alex: "I know you were prepared to stand up to him, my dear, but that would have been quite unnecessary. I discovered that he owned a string of sex shops—lawyers are forbidden to own businesses, did you know that—and I would have brought that to the attention of the court. He never posed a real danger."

"Oh, Uncle Richard, why didn't you tell me? I've been so worried."

"I guess I felt that since I had worked things out, you had no need to know the sordid details. Perhaps I was mistaken."

Eugene shook his head in disbelief, "Well done," he said to Richard. *He's a wily old fox. I wonder what else he thinks we have no need to know.*

CHAPTER SEVENTY-THREE

FRANÇOIS TRAN MET THEM AT the station at Nîmes and drove them back to Trubenne. Soon a pot of *Poulet Marengo* was simmering on the stove. Alex had adopted Charlotte's practice of cooking a large batch of food and freezing some of it, to be table-ready later on.

"I've meant to ask if you've spoken to Bruno?" she said as they sat down to eat dinner.

"Yeah, Bruno said he remembered that Jacques has a house in Montenegro, and he thought he could be there."

"Where in Montenegro, did he say?"

"Nope. That's the problem. He doesn't remember. Does that sound familiar?"

Richard had been trying to trim the last pieces of flesh from a drumstick. Frustrated, he picked it up in his hands to finish it off. When his mouth was empty, he wiped his fingers on his napkin: "Are you talking about Jacques Mornnais?"

"Sorry uncle Richard, yes, we are. Eugene thinks Jacques may have some information on a few of his family members in Ukraine. He'd like to talk to him, but Jacques has disappeared."

"I remember John Royston talking about him one day. He said—it was just in passing, really—that Mornnais liked to collect homes. He had one in the south of France near Saint Raphael, but I don't think he mentioned the name of the town. And another in Montenegro of all places. So, your friend Bruno is right. What struck me, though, was Royston saying that not only did Mornnais own a home there, but he had bought the entire village. A place called Berici or maybe Perici, something like that. So perhaps you ought to look for him in Montenegro."

"Berici or Perici, did you say? I know almost nothing about Montenegro, except for what Bruno said, and it looks like I'm going to learn a whole lot more. Thanks for the tip, Richard." *The old guy is full of surprises. Wouldn't I like to get inside his memory?*

He didn't need Bruno after all. He could go after Jacques by himself.

EPILOGUE

IN MID-SEPTEMBER, PATRICK TRABERT GOT a phone call from a man who said he was a friend of Momo. Patrick borrowed Véronique's car and drove to Nemours. He was instructed to go to the same café where Nicolas Pagès had met Bruno in January 2010, although there was no way Patrick could have known that. Momo's friend was waiting for Patrick. He stood up and introduced himself: "Hi, I'm Julian."

Unlike Momo, Julian wore a suit; his shirt collar was open to reveal a gold chain that glittered against his dark skin. His teeth had a yellowish tinge. Patrick wished that they were white; it would have gone better with the suit and the gold chain.

"So, Patrick, I hear that you had a little problem in Aigues-Mortes, but not to worry, it's been taken care of."

"Oh, that's great," said Patrick. He didn't want to know anything more.

They ordered coffee, did he want anything else, Julian asked him.

"No, I'm good, thanks."

"Okay, then, to get to the point. We have an import-export business in Mauritius, and we'd like it if you'd work with us. I mean, your girlfriend is an antiques dealer, right, and we'd like it if you could import our furniture."

Patrick wondered how Julian knew about Véronique, but then he remembered that Bruno knew all about the Pagès family business.

"Are you with me, Patrick?"

"Oh, yes."

"Good. It's quite simple. You'll take delivery of the furniture, and then someone will come by your gallery to purchase some of the articles and take them away. We'll be sure that you make a nice profit on the sale."

Patrick looked down at his coffee cup while Julian smiled his yellow-toothed smile.

"Have you got it, then, Patrick?"

"Uh, yes, but I'll need to talk to my girlfriend, it's her business, you know."

"Yes, you do that. We're counting on you to explain how this is a win-win situation, with no risks like you had in Aigues-Mortes."

Julian looked at his watch. It had a dark brown crocodile leather band and a large face with several dials. Patrick didn't recognize it—he used his cell phone to tell time—but it looked expensive.

"Sorry, but I gotta run now. Nice to meet you, Patrick. We'll be in touch."

Patrick turned to watch Julian leave the café. He caught a glimpse of the pointed toes of his shiny shoes. He remembered when Bruno had beaten him in Marseille, and now he imagined those shiny shoes kicking him in the ribs, as Bruno had done. That image was chased by another scenario: he imagined that he had told Véronique about Julian's offer, and she threw him out of the house.

He asked the waiter for a glass of water to settle his stomach. He gulped it down and slowly drove back to Fontainebleau, just as Nicolas Pagès had done months ago.

When Patrick had returned to the house, he unburdened himself to Véronique. He told her the truth about the events at Aigues-Mortes, about Bruno, who had given him the roll of bills and had arranged for Julian to call, and about his meeting with Julian. Patrick felt more than relief; he was free now that the burden of half-truths and lies lifted. He had packed his belongings and prepared himself for the onslaught of her anger before she threw him out.

Her reaction startled him.

"Patrick, stop looking down at the floor. I guess you think I'd be pissed off, right?"

"Uh, well, you've been in a bad mood lately."

"That's because pretty soon I'm going to run out of stuff to sell. And then what? Can you imagine me working my butt off in some office, sitting in front of a computer screen all day? No way, my friend. You can tell Julian I want to meet him, the sooner, the better."

# # #

It was now October, and the first shipment of furniture had arrived. Julian came by to show them which pieces to unpack and display. The other tables and chairs would be picked up by the purchaser.

"You remember that guy Filippo?"

Patrick's stomach clenched.

"Uh, yeah. Why do you ask?"

"He shouldn't have opened that bag of rice. You don't want to make the same mistake."

Before Patrick could respond, Véronique cut in: "Do you think we're stupid or what? Just be sure that you don't mess up the pick-ups."

Julian smiled; while Patrick was a limp noodle, his girlfriend was just the kind of partner they needed.

# # #

Phuket

After work, Caroline Trabert went to meet friends at a bar just up the street from the bookshop where she worked. The rainy monsoon season would be over soon, but now she hurried to avoid the usual evening shower. She was early, the place not yet crowded with tourists and the after-work crowd.

As Caroline savored the taste of a cold Thai beer, she felt as if someone was staring at her. Caroline had accepted the fact that she was no longer an attractive woman (had she ever been, she wondered) and looked around to see if her imagination was working overtime. An Asian man, a smile on his waxy, pockmarked face, was coming to her table.

"Hello, you're Patrick's mom, aren't you?"

"Well, if it isn't Mr. Joe. So nice to see you again."

"Do you mind if I join you for a few minutes?"

"I'm expecting some friends…" She didn't want Joe talking about Patrick and importing rice or whatever it was that he did in front of her friends.

"Yes, of course. I won't keep you. I just wanted to tell you how pleased we are with Patrick and his girlfriend."

Patrick. Theirs was a transactional relationship; he would call and ask for money, she would complain and transfer funds. Since he hadn't asked for money since July, she assumed that his job in Aigues-Mortes had worked out. *What has that snippy girl got to do with anything?* She wondered.

"His girlfriend?"

"Oh yes, hasn't he told you? Naughty boy! His girlfriend is an antiques dealer, I guess you know that, and she and Patrick have become furniture importers. It fits right in with her business. They make a good team."

First rice, now furniture. What have I gotten Patrick into? Oh well, if he's making a go of it, who am I to complain? At least he's not whining about money.

"I'm so glad to hear that, Joe. If you'll excuse me, I see my friends are just coming through the door."

Caroline took her beer and got up to meet her friends. She would have to find another favorite bar. She didn't care to run into Joe again, although she couldn't say why. Another thought crossed her mind as she walked towards her friends: it would have been nice for Patrick to call even if he was not short of money. But when you came down to it, what else did they have to talk about?

# # #

Toulouse

Bruno turned his collar up and hunched his head down between his shoulders, like an old tortoise. The weather in Toulouse was crazy: two days ago, it had been like summer, and now he could see clouds of his breath in the chill morning air.

Bruno was making up for lost time. He now had a different woman almost every night. He picked them up in different clubs, but he remained sober and drug-free and avoided the violent behavior of his time working for Jacques.

He made sure to remember their names; otherwise, they were merely recipients for his newly returned sexual desire. He never invited them back to his apartment. He told them his name was Emile Duval and that he had grown up in Paris. When he wasn't fucking, he was studying the books on Montenegro. He focused on trying to recognize the town where Jacques had his house. Once he'd done that, Bruno would disappear from Toulouse for good, leaving no traces behind him.

As he walked down Rue des Arts, he saw a police car parked in front of his building. He continued without quickening his pace. At the corner, he turned right onto Rue Croix Baragnon and went into a coffee shop near the Carmes market, where he hung around for an hour. Had the police identified the guy he'd thrown into the rubbish bin? He'd hoped that the body would have gone directly into the incinerator, but perhaps it hadn't. He went back to Rue des Arts, and when he saw that the police car had gone, he slipped into the building and went up to his apartment, packed up his books and clothing and left.

He had paid his rent to the end of the month; he left the keys on the table and slammed the door shut behind him. For a moment he didn't remember the name he'd used to rent the apartment; ah yes, Bruno Leblanc. He called the rental agency and left a message that he'd had to go to Paris on an assignment and that he wouldn't be renewing his lease. There was no way to tie him to the murder of that noisy asshole, but Bruno preferred to avoid any contact with the police: you never knew where that could lead, certainly no place good.

He walked to the train station. An occasional raindrop fell from the dark, damp sky, but he didn't notice it. His sister Sandra had kept her apartment in Lyon when she left France and that would make a discreet hideaway while he continued studying the towns of Montenegro.

It didn't take long to settle into Sandra's flat. Should he stop by Chez Michel to pick up his sister's mail? He was sure that by now, no one would be contacting Sandra. Instead, he walked through Les Pentes and continued up the hill to Croix-Rousse. He liked to walk through the market there; the colors and smells were one of his few happy childhood memories.

He stopped at a stall selling roast chickens; he'd buy one along with some potatoes for his lunch. He waited his turn, gazing aimlessly down the crowded sidewalk. A cloud of red hair caught his attention: it was the red-haired cow, the one with the restaurant where he'd seen his face in the mural that the Chinese painters had done. Bruno smirked. It would be amusing to let her know that he'd seen Li, and he left his place in line and started walking towards her.

"Marie-Agnès," he called out. At that moment the crowd melted away from him, like the tide running out, leaving Marie-Agnès alone on the shore. He heard screams, saw an arm wielding a bloody knife emerge from the moving sea of bodies. The man was inches away from Marie-Agnès when Bruno pushed her to the ground. He felt the soft fabric of her wool coat, smelled her freshly shampooed hair, saw the slender fingers of one hand splayed on the pavement. The knife missed Marie-Agnès neck but cut a gash in Bruno's head.

"*Allahu akbar*." The cry rang out in the market. As the attacker ran down the sidewalk an old woman pushed her market caddy into his path. He stumbled, bringing down upon him a table with sacks of potatoes. He might have been lynched by the sellers in the market, but for the intervention of the police.

Marie-Agnès joined the injured in the ambulances that soon arrived. At the hospital, she looked for Bruno and found him on a stretcher in the corridor, waiting to be treated. She leaned over him; his head was wrapped in bloodstained bandages.

"Bruno, thank you, you saved my life."

His eyes met hers, and he moved his head slightly from one side to the other.

"Okay, I won't say that I know you."

She felt tears well up: "You'll be all right, I know that."

His lips moved, and she brought her head closer to his.

"What did you say?"

"I'm sorry," he whispered, and his eyes closed.

What was he sorry for? For having sent Jacques' henchmen after her, or for the myriad other acts that had composed his life? Marie-Agnès chose to believe that he was sorry for what he had tried to do to her, but she would never know for sure.

# # #

Trubenne

Eugene had been quieter than usual. The gold flecks still danced in his eyes when he smiled, but he seemed more subdued, more reflective. Richard's bombshell—the offhand announcement that Jacques Mornnais owned a village in Montenegro—had disturbed him.

Until today, his quest to discover the identities of his biological parents existed in his imagination only. But now, it had suddenly become real: he knew where to find the man who might have some of the answers. Alex's words echoed in his head: "If you want to find out about your birth parents, you need to find a way to talk to Jacques." He felt the little pinpricks of doubt: was he sure that he wanted to hear what Jacques might say? Why had he come across that damned letter among Madeleine's papers? And why had he kept Jacques' file labeled Ukraine? Alex came up behind him and put her arms around his chest, leaning her head against his back.

"Are you okay?" she said, her voice barely audible. "You've not been very talkative as of late."

"Yes, I'm good. Listen, I've been thinking, I need to visit Jacques, take care of things once and for all. Are you up for a trip to Montenegro?"

She tightened her arms, "yes, of course," she whispered.

THE END

A FORGERY IN TOULOUSE

OUR PLAYERS

Antoine Tipette, a management consultant

Bruno Edremal, recovered amnesiac

Eugene Spector, an FBI agent on leave from the Bureau

Father Paul, a priest

Father Joseph, the priest-in-residence

Jacqueline Fitzgerald, her marriage has broken up

Li Xio (Ma Zhen), a Chinese art forger who worked for Jacques Mornnais

Marie-Agnès Duvalois, (Mag) a childhood friend of Alex Thornhill

Patrick Trabert, an aimless young man

<u>Vesla de Trubenne Family</u>

Alexia Chase Thornhill (Alex), Renovating the family château at Trubenne

Richard Vesla de Trubenne, Alex's Granduncle

Charlotte Vesla de Trubenne, Alex's cousin, murdered by Jacques Mornnais' thugs

Vital Vesla de Trubenne, Alex's cousin

SUPPORTING ROLES

Anne Vesla de Trubenne, Vital's wife

Barbara Tomason (Babs), rents out her apartment for confidential meetings

Caroline Trabert, Patrick Trabert's mother

Charles Paoli, Sauveur Paoli's cousin

Dominic Monteil, owner of the DM Animal Hotel & Spa

Ella, Jacques' former housekeeper at Château d'Hélène

Emma, Max Martolla's wife

Filippo, the chef at Citadel Sushi

François Tran, a handyman at Trubenne

Jacques Mornnais, publisher of the lifestyle magazine *Artixia*

Jean-Paul (JP) & Roger, drivers

Joe, a man Caroline Trabert encounters in Phuket

Kenneth Petit, works at the French intelligence agency

Kate Spector, Eugene Spector's sister

Madeleine Connors, a friend of Eugene Spector's family

Max Martolla, owner of Citadel Sushi

Merv Peters, an American practicing law in Paris, died in an automobile accident

Michel, owner of the café Chez Michel

Michel de Clermont d'Auvergne, a security consultant

Momo, works for a rice importer

Novices, live at the *Résidence*

Raymond Chartrier, Li's agent

Samih Ceckin, a trash collector

Sauveur Paoli, a real estate lawyer murdered by Jacques Mornnais' thugs

Simone Vesla de Trubenne, Vital's wife

Tarek, Jacques' driver, killed in an automobile accident

Tomas, Mag's companion

Travis Bartlett & his wife Julie, Eugene's friends who live in Lyon

Véronique Pagès, the daughter of Nicholas Pagès, an art dealer who was murdered

Viktor, Madeleine Connors' brother

Wen, a Chinese art forger who worked for Jacques Mornnais

CASTLE BRIDGE MEDIA RECOMMENDS...

If you liked this book, you might also enjoy reading the following titles from Castle Bridge Media available on Amazon or by order at your favorite book store:

The 23rd Hero
By Rebecca Anne Nguyen

ANIMAL CHARMER
By Rain Nox
Animal Charmer
Magic & Melody

Austinites
By In Churl Yo

Bloodsucker City
By Jim Towns

SOUL CATCHER
By Don Sawyer
The Burning Gem
The Tunnels of Buda

THE CASTLE OF HORROR ANTHOLOGY SERIES
Volume 1
Volume 2: *Holiday Horrors*
Volume 3: *Scary Summer Stories*
Volume 4: *Women Running From Houses*
Volume 5: *Thinly Veiled: The 70s*
Volume 6: *Femme Fatales**
Volume 7: *Love Gone Wrong*
Volume 8: *Thinly Veiled: The 80s*
Volume 9: *Young Adult*
Volume 10: *Thinly Veiled: Saturday Mournings*
Volume 11: *Revenge*
Volume 12: *Ripped From The Headlines*
Edited By Jason Henderson and In Churl Yo
*Edited By P.J. Hoover

Child of Dark Water
By E.G. Rand

Castle of Horror Podcast Book of Great Horror: Our Favorites, Top Tens and Bizarre Pleasures
Edited By Jason Henderson

Cherry Dark
By R.L. Wilburn

Dream State
By Martin Ott

Dominic
By Lee Guzman

FRENCH DECEPTION
By Janice Nagourney
A Forgery in Paris
A Forgery in Lyon
A Forgery in Marseille

FuturePast Sci-Fi Anthology
Edited by In Churl Yo

GLAZIER'S GAP
Ghosts of the Forbidden
By Leanna Renee Hieber

Hellfall
By Jay Gould

Isonation
By In Churl Yo

JAYU CITY CHRONICLES
By Chris M. Arnone
The Hermes Protocol
Necropolis Alpha

Junk Film: Why Bad Movies Matter
By Katharine Coldiron

Nightwalkers: Gothic Horror Movies
By Bruce Lanier Wright

MID-LIFE CRISIS THRILLERS
18 Miles From Town
By Jason Henderson
Lost Angel
By Sam Knight

Ties That Kill
By Deven Greene

THE PATH
By David Bowles
The Blue-Spangled Blue
The Deepest Green

Strange Shape of Love
By Herta Feely

SURF MYSTIC
By Peyton Douglas
Night of the Book Man
Dark of the Curl

The Thing That Happened When We Were Little
By Caroline Kelly Franklin

Tick Town
By Christopher A. Micklos

Yesterday's Tomorrows: The Golden Age of Science Fiction Movies
By Bruce Lanier Wright

Please remember to leave us your reviews on Amazon and Goodreads!

THANK YOU FOR SUPPORTING INDEPENDENT PUBLISHERS AND AUTHORS!
castlebridgemedia.com

www.ingramcontent.com/pod-product-compliance
Lightning Source LLC
Chambersburg PA
CBHW020136120726
47903CB00007B/2281
9798994041000